I opened the door as quietly as I could and looked inside.

She was awake and looking at me. Her face was calm, her eyes expressionless. Her eyes moved down to my right hand, which was gripping a dagger. She didn't seem frightened.

She sat up. The blue nightgown was intended to be modest, but it was also intended for Dragaerans, so it fell rather low on her. Her eyes traveled from the dagger to my face. We studied each other for a time, then I forced my hand to relax, and release its grip on the weapon.

Dammit! *I* was the one who was armed, *she* was the one who was helpless. There was no reason for *me* to be afraid of *her*. . . .

"Watch Steven Brust. He's good. He moves fast. He surprises you. Watching him untangle the diverse threads of intrigue, honor, character and mayhem from amid the gears of a world as intricately constructed as a Swiss watch is a rare pleasure.

"I like this book a lot. I recommend it."

—Roger Zelazny

Ace books by Steven Brust

JHEREG
YENDI
TO REIGN IN HELL (coming in May '85)

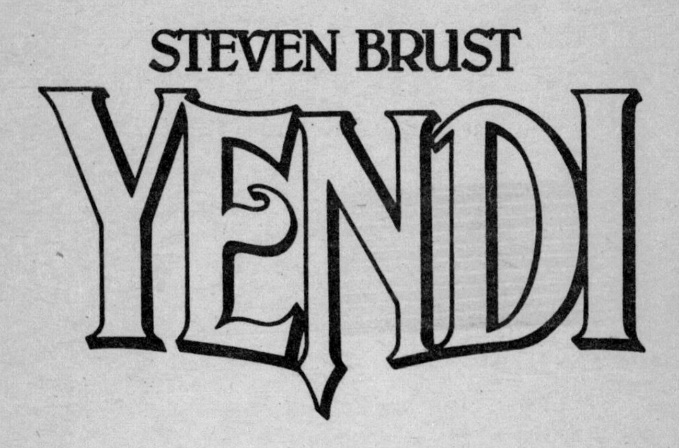
STEVEN BRUST
YENDI

ACE FANTASY BOOKS
NEW YORK

YENDI

An Ace Fantasy Book / published by arrangement with
the author and the author's agent, Valerie Smith

PRINTING HISTORY
Ace Original / July 1984
Second printing / October 1984

Cover art by Stephen Hickman

For information address: The Berkley Publishing Group,
200 Madison Avenue, New York, New York 10016.

ISBN: 0-441-94457-4

Ace Fantasy Books are published by The Berkley Publishing Group,
200 Madison Avenue, New York, New York 10016.
PRINTED IN THE UNITED STATES OF AMERICA

This is for Reen and Corwin and Aliera and Carolyn and for my father-in-law Bill

Wellock's Area

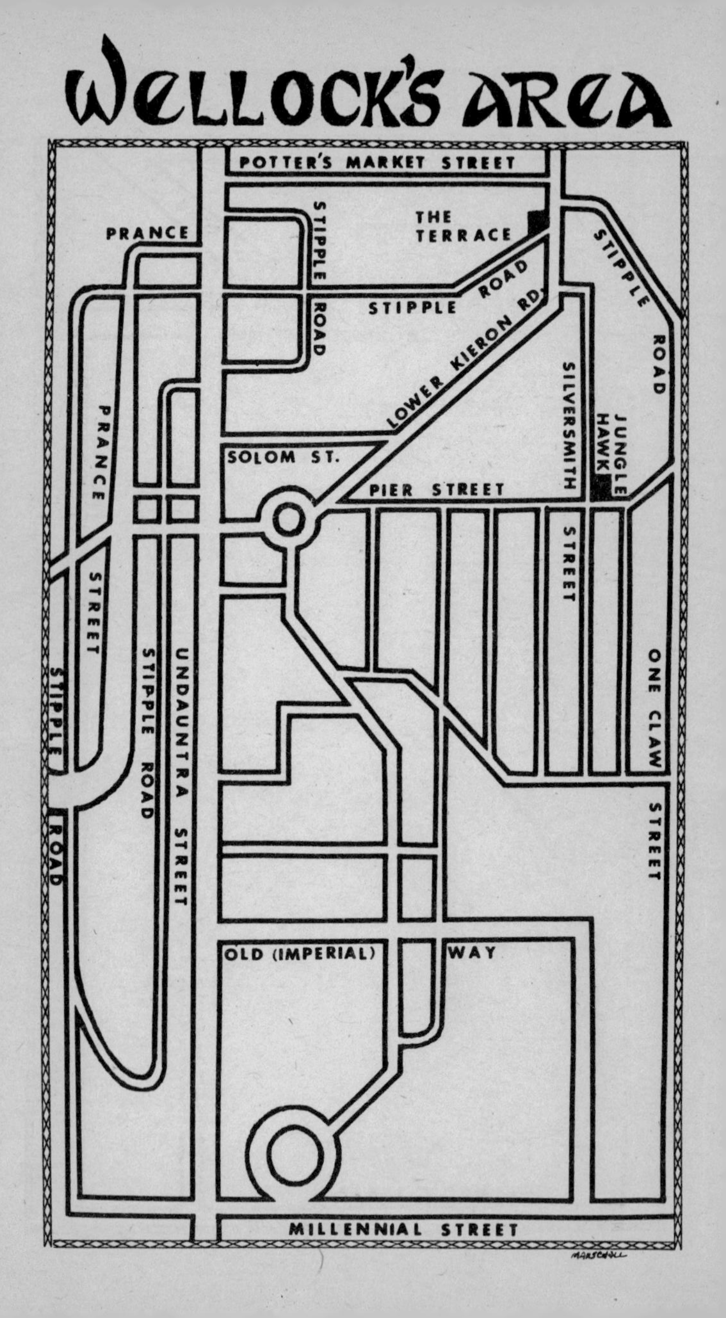

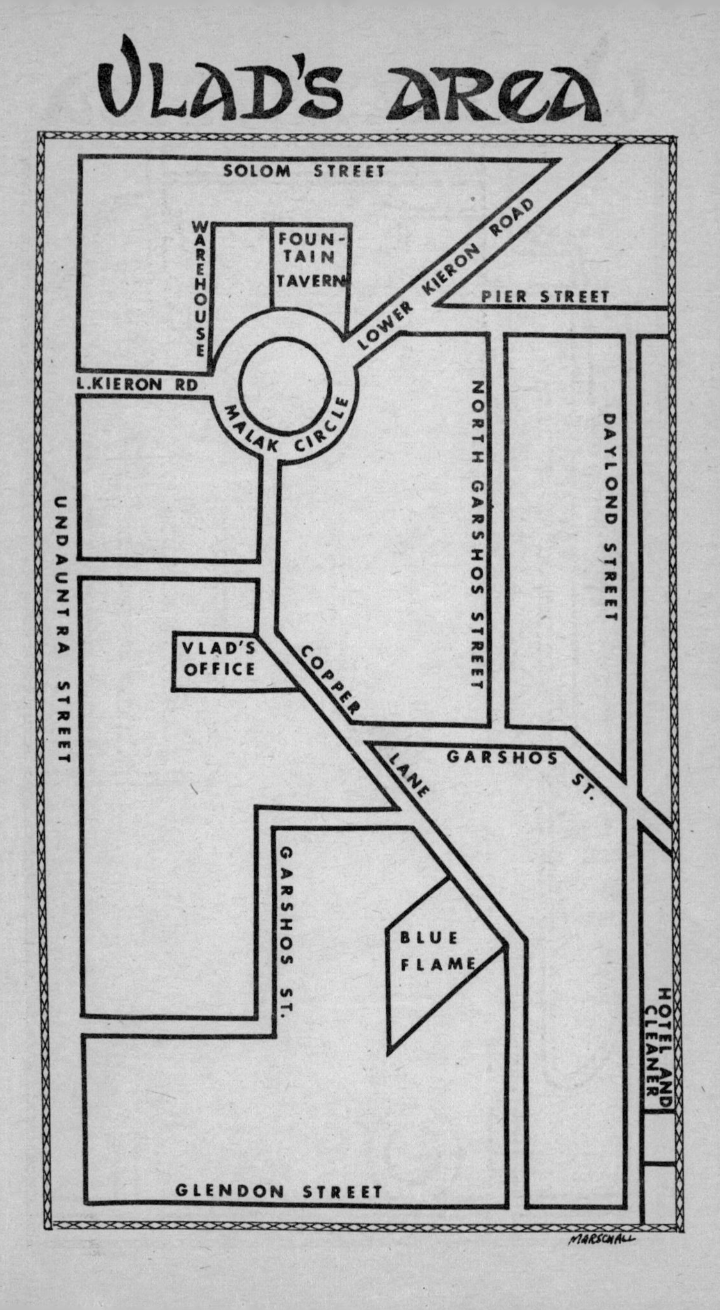
VLAD'S AREA
SOLOM STREET
WAREHOUSE
FOUN-
TAIN
TAVERN
LOWER KIERON ROAD
PIER STREET
L.KIERON RD
MALAK CIRCLE
NORTH GARSHOS STREET
DAYLOND STREET
UNDAUNTRA STREET
VLAD'S
OFFICE
COPPER
LANE
GARSHOS
ST.
GARSHOS ST.
BLUE
FLAME
HOTEL AND
CLEANER
GLENDON STREET
MARSCHALL

Introduction

When I was young, I was taught that every citizen of the Dragaeran Empire was born into one of the seventeen Great Houses, each named for an animal. I was taught that humans, or "Easterners," such as I, were worthless scum. I was taught that the only choices we had, if we wished to amount to anything, were to swear fealty to some lord and become part of the peasant class in the House of the Teckla, or, as my father did, buy Orders of Nobility in the House of the Jhereg.

Later, I found a wild jhereg, and trained him, and set about to leave my mark on Dragaeran society.

When I was older, I learned that most of what I had been taught were lies.

The Cycle

Phoenix sinks into decay
Haughty dragon yearns to slay.
Lyorn growls and lowers horn
Tiassa dreams and plots are born.
Hawk looks down from lofty flight
Dzur stalks and blends with night.
Issola strikes from courtly bow
Tsalmoth maintains though none knows
  how.
Vallista rends and then rebuilds
Jhereg feeds on others' kills.
Quiet iorich won't forget
Sly chreotha weaves his net.
Yendi coils and strikes, unseen
Orca circles, hard and lean.
Frightened teckla hides in grass
Jhegaala shifts as moments pass
Athyra rules minds' interplay
Phoenix rise from ashes, gray.

1

"Stay out of sight, in case they get rude."

Kragar says that life is like an onion, but he doesn't mean the same thing by it that I do.

He talks about peeling it, and how you can go deeper and deeper, until finally you get to the center and nothing is there. I suppose there's truth in that, but in the years when my father ran a restaurant, I never peeled an onion, I chopped them; Kragar's analogy doesn't do much for me.

When I say that life is like an onion, I mean this: if you don't do anything with it, it goes rotten. So far, that's no different from other vegetables. But when an onion goes bad, it can do it from either the inside, or the outside. So sometimes you get one that looks good, but the core is rotten. Other times, you can see a bad spot on it, but if you cut that out, the rest is fine. Tastes sharp, but that's what you paid for, isn't it?

Dzurlords like to fancy themselves as pantry chefs who go around cutting the rotten parts out of onions. Trouble is, they generally can't tell the good from the bad. Dragonlords are good at finding bad spots, but when they find one they like to throw out the whole barrelful. A Hawklord will find a bad spot every time. He'll watch you cook the thing, and eat it, and he'll nod sagaciously when you spit it out again. If you ask why he didn't tell you about it, he'll look startled and say, "You didn't ask."

I could go on, but what's the point? In the House Jhereg, we don't care teckla droppings about bad spots. We're just here to sell onions.

But sometimes someone will pay me to remove a bad spot. This had earned me thirty-two hundred gold Imperials that day, and to let the tension drain out I visited the more or less permanent party at the keep of the Lord Morrolan. I was sort of on his staff, as a security consultant, which gave me a standing invitation.

Lady Teldra let me in as I recovered from the teleport and I made my way to the banquet hall. I studied the mass of humanity (I use the term loosely) from the doorway, looking for familiar faces, and soon spotted the tall form of Morrolan himself.

Guests who didn't know me watched as I moved toward him; some made remarks intended for me to overhear. I always attract attention at Morrolan's parties—because I'm the only Jhereg there; because I'm the only "Easterner" (read: "human") there; or because I walk in with my jhereg familiar, Loiosh, riding on my shoulder.

"Nice party," I told Morrolan.

"Where are the trays of dead teckla, then?" said Loiosh psionically.

"Thank you, Vlad. It pleases me that you are here."

Morrolan always talks like that. I think he can't help it.

We wandered over to a table where one of his servants was pouring out small draughts of various wines, commenting on them as he did. I got a glass of red Darloscha and sipped it. Nice and dry, but it would have been better chilled. Dragaerans don't understand wine.

"Good evening Vlad; Morrolan."

I turned and bowed low to Aliera e'Kieron, Morrolan's

cousin and Dragon Heir to the Throne. Morrolan bowed and squeezed her hand. I smiled. "Good evening, Aliera. Any duels, yet?"

"Why yes," she said. "Did you hear?"

"As a matter of fact, no; I was being facetious. You really do have a duel lined up?"

"Yes, for tomorrow. Some teckla of a Dzurlord noticed how I walk and made remarks."

I shook my head and tsked. "What's his name?"

She shrugged. "I don't know. I'll find out tomorrow. Morrolan, have you seen Sethra?"

"No. I assume she is at Dzur Mountain. Perhaps she will show up later. Is it important?"

"Not really. I think I've isolated a new e'Mondaar recessive. It'll wait."

"*I* am interested," said Morrolan. "Would you be pleased to tell me of it?"

"I'm not sure what it is yet . . ." said Aliera. The two of them walked off. Well, Morrolan walked. Aliera, who was the shortest Dragaeran I've ever met, levitated, her long, silver-blue dress running along the ground to hide the fact. Aliera had golden hair and green eyes—usually. Although she wasn't carrying it now, she also had a sword that was longer than she was. She had taken the sword from the hand of Kieron the Conquerer, the head of her line, in the Paths of the Dead. There's a story in there, too, but never mind.

Anyway, they walked away, and I drew on my link with the Imperial Orb, did a small sorcery spell, and chilled the wine. I sipped it again. Much better.

"The problem for tonight, Loiosh, is: how am I going to get laid?"

"Boss, sometimes you disgust me."

"Tell me about it."

"Aside from that, if you own four brothels—"

"I've decided I don't like visiting brothels."

"Eh? Why not?"

"You wouldn't understand."

"Try me."

"All right. Put it this way: sex with Dragaerans feels more than half like bestiality, anyway. With whores, it feels like paying the . . . whatever."

"Go on, boss. Finish the sentence. Now I'm curious."

"Oh, shut up."

"What is it about killing someone that makes you so horny, anyway?"

"Got me."

"You need a wife."

"Go to Deathsgate."

"We did that once, remember?"

"Yeah. And I remember how you felt about the giant jhereg there."

"Don't start on that, boss."

"Then shut up about my sex life."

"You brought it up."

There was nothing to say to that, so I let it drop. I sipped my wine again, and felt that peculiar, nagging sensation of there's-something-I-ought-to-be-thinking-about that heralds someone trying to reach me psionically. I quickly found a quiet corner and opened up my mind for contact.

"How's the party, boss?"

"Not bad, Kragar. What's up that can't wait for morning?"

"Your bootblack is here. He's going to be made Issola Heir to the Throne tomorrow, so he's finishing up his calls."

"Funny. What is it really?"

"A question. Did you open up a new gambling joint in Malak Circle?"

"Of course not. You'd have heard about it long ago."

"That's what I thought. Then there's a problem."

"I see. Some punk thinking we won't notice? Or is somebody trying to muscle in?"

"It looks professional, Vlad. He's got protection there."

"How many?"

"Three. And I know one of them. He's done 'work.'"

"Oh."

"What do you think?"

"Kragar, you know how a chamber pot gets when it isn't

emptied for a few days?"

"Yeah?"

"And you know how, when you finally do empty it, there's all that stuff stuck on the bottom?"

"Yeah?"

"Well, that stuff on the bottom is how I feel about this."

"Gotcha."

"I'll be right over."

I found Morrolan in a corner with Aliera and a tall Dragaeran who had the facial features of the House of the Athyra and was dressed all in forest green. She looked down at me, figuratively and literally. It's frustrating being both a Jhereg and an Easterner—people sneer at you for both reasons.

"Vlad," said Morrolan, "this is the Sorceress in Green. Sorceress, this is Baronet Vladimir Taltos."

She nodded, almost imperceptibly. I bowed with a deep flourish, dragging the back of my hand over the floor, bringing it up over my head, and saying, "Gentle lady, I am every bit as charmed to meet you as you are to meet me."

She sniffed and looked away.

Aliera's eyes were twinkling.

Morrolan looked troubled, then shrugged.

"Sorceress in Green," I said. "I've never met an Athyra who wasn't a sorcerer, and the green I can see, so I can't say the title tells me—"

"That will be sufficient, Vlad," said Morrolan. "And she isn't—"

"Sorry. I wanted to tell you that something's come up. I'm afraid I'll have to leave." I turned to the Sorceress. "I'm sorry to do this to you, my dear, but try not to let it ruin your evening."

She looked back at me and smiled sweetly. "How would you," she said, "like to be a newt?"

Loiosh hissed.

"I asked you to desist, Vlad," said Morrolan sharply.

I dropped it. "I'll be leaving, then," I said, bowing my head.

"Very well. If there's anything I can do, let me know."

I nodded. Unfortunately for him, I remembered the remark.

Do you know what the single biggest difference between a Dragaeran and an Easterner is? It isn't that they are so much taller and stronger than we are; I'm living proof that size and strength aren't that important. It isn't that they live two or three thousand years compared to our fifty or sixty; in the crowd I hang around with, no one expects to die of old age anyway. It isn't even that they have a natural link with the Imperial Orb that allows them to use sorcery; Easterners (such as my late, unlamented father) can buy titles in the House of the Jhereg, or swear fealty to some noble, move out to the countryside and become a Teckla—thereby becoming citizens and getting the link.

No, the biggest difference that I've found is this: a Dragaeran can teleport without feeling sick to his stomach afterwards.

I arrived in the street outside my office about ready to throw up. I took a few deep breaths and waited while my gut settled down. I had had one of Morrolan's sorcerers do the actual spell. I can do it myself, but I'm not very good; a rough landing makes things even worse.

My offices at this time were on Copper Lane, in back of a small gambling operation, which was in back of a psychedelic herb shop. My offices consisted of three rooms. One was a screening room, where Melestav, my receptionist-bodyguard, sat. To his right was Kragar's office and the files, and behind Melestav was my actual office. Kragar had a small desk and one hard wooden chair—there wasn't room for anything else. The screening room had four chairs that were almost comfortable. My desk was a bit bigger than Kragar's, smaller than Melestav's, and had a well-padded swivel chair facing the door. Next to the door were two comfortable chairs, one of which would be occupied by Kragar when he showed up.

I told Melestav to let Kragar know I was in and sat down at my desk to wait.

"Uh, boss?"

"Oh." I sighed as I realized that, once again, Kragar had sneaked in without my seeing him. He claims that he doesn't do it on purpose—that he's just naturally sneaky.

"What have you found out, Kragar?"

"Nothing I didn't tell you before."

"Okay. Let's go blow some money."

"Both of us?"

"No. You stay out of sight, in case they get rude."

"Okay."

As we went out I ran a hand through my hair. This let me rub my arm against the right side of my cloak, so I could make sure that various pieces of hardware were in place. With my left hand I adjusted the collar, letting me check a few more on that side.

Out on the street, I gave a quick look around, then walked the block and a half up to Malak Circle. Copper Lane is what is called a one-and-a-half-cart street, which makes it wider than many. The buildings are packed tightly together, and most of them have windows only on the upper stories. Malak Circle is a turnaround, with a fountain that hasn't worked as long as I can remember. Copper Lane ends there. Lower Kieron Road enters from the left as you approach from Copper Lane, and leaves again, slightly wider, ahead, and to the right.

"Okay, Kragar," I said, "where—" I stopped. "Kragar?"

"Right in front of you, boss."

"Oh. Where is it?"

"First door to the left of the Fountain Tavern. Inside, up the stairs, and to the right."

"Okay. Stay alert."

"Check."

"Loiosh, try to find a window you can look in. If not, just stay in touch."

"Right, boss." He flew off.

I went in, up a narrow stairway with no handrail, and came to the top. I took a deep breath, checked my weapons once more, and clapped.

The door opened at once. The guy who stood there was dressed in black and gray for House Jhereg, and had a broadsword strapped to his side. He was damn near seven and a half feet tall and broader than is usual for a Dragaeran. He loooked down at me and said, "Sorry, Whiskers. Humans only," and shut the door. Dragaerans often seem confused about who the "humans" are.

Being called "Whiskers" didn't bother me—I'd deliberately grown a mustache because Dragaerans can't. But to be shut out of a game that shouldn't even be here without my permission displeased me immensely.

I quickly checked the door and found that it was bound with sorcery. I gave a flick of my right wrist and Spellbreaker, two feet of thin gold chain, came into my hand. I lashed out at the door and felt the spell fail. I put the chain away as the door was flung open again.

The guy's eyes narrowed and he started moving toward me. I smiled at him. "I'd like to speak to the proprietor, if I may."

"I see," he said, "that you're going to need help getting down the stairs." He moved toward me again.

I shook my head. "It's sad that you can't cooperate with a simple request, dead man."

He moved in, and my right sleeve dagger was in my hand. Then I was past him, ducking under his arms. Six inches of steel were buried, at an upward angle, between his fourth and fifth ribs, twisted to notch on the sternum. I stepped into the room as I heard vague moaning and coughing noises from behind me, followed by the sound of a falling body. Contrary to popular myth, the guy would probably remain alive for over an hour. But contrary to another popular myth, he would be in shock and so wouldn't be able to do anything to keep himself alive.

The room was small, with only one window. There were three tables of s'yang stones in action, one with five players, the other two with four. Most of the players seemed to be Teckla, a couple of Jhereg, and there was one Tsalmoth. There were two other Jhereg there, just as Kragar had told me, who seemed to be working for the place. They were both moving at me quickly, one was drawing his sword. Oh me, oh my.

I put a table between myself and one of them, then kicked it over toward him. At that moment, the window broke and Loiosh flew straight at the other. I could forget about that guy for a few minutes, anyway.

The one I'd kicked the table at, scattering coins and stones and customers, stumbled a bit. I drew my rapier and cut his wrist as his arm was flailing around in front of me. He dropped the blade, and I stepped in and kicked him between the legs. He moaned and doubled over. I brought the pommel of my blade down on his head and he dropped.

I moved to the other one. *"Enough, Loiosh. Let him alone, and watch my back."*

"Right, boss."

The guy tried to get his blade out as I approached and Loiosh left him, but mine was already out. I touched his throat with the point and smiled. "I'd like to speak to the manager," I said.

He stopped moving. He looked at me coldly, with no trace of fear in his eyes. "He's not here."

"Tell me who he is and you'll live," I said. "Don't, and you'll die."

He remained silent. I moved the point of my blade up until it was opposite his left eye. The threat was clear: if his brain was destroyed, he wouldn't be in any condition to be revivified. There was still no sign of fear, but he said, "Laris."

"Thank you," I told him. "Lie down on the floor."

He did so. I turned to the customers. "This place is closed," I said. They began heading for the door.

At that moment, there was a woosh of displaced air, and five more Jhereg were in the room, swords drawn. Oops. Without a word being spoken, Loiosh was on my shoulder.

"Kragar, take off."

"Right."

I drew recklessly on my link and tried to teleport, but failed. I sometimes wish teleport blocks could be outlawed. I lunged at one of them, scattered a handful of sharp pointy things with my left hand, and jumped through the already broken window. I heard cursing sounds behind me.

I tried a quick levitation spell, which must have worked a little bit since landing didn't hurt. I kept moving, in case they had sharp pointy things, too. I tried the teleport again, and it worked.

I found myself on my back, right outside the door to the shop containing my offices. I threw up.

I climbed to my feet, dusted off my cloak, and went inside. The proprietor was looking at me curiously.

"There's a mess on the street outside," I told him. "Clean it up."

"Laris, eh boss?" said Kragar a bit later. "One of our next-door neighbors. He controls about ten square blocks. He only has a couple of operations that face our territory, so far."

I put my feet up on my desk. "More than twice as much area as I have," I mused.

"It looked like he was expecting trouble, didn't it?"

I nodded. "So, is he just testing us, or is he really trying to move in on me?"

Kragar shrugged. "Hard to say for sure, but I think he wants to move in."

"Okay," I said, sounding a lot calmer than I felt. "Can we talk him out of it, or is it war?"

"Are we up to a war?"

"Of course not," I snapped. "I've only had my own area for half a year. We should have been expecting something like this. Damn."

He nodded.

I took a deep breath. "Okay, how many enforcers do we have on our payroll?"

"Six, not counting the ones who are permanently assigned to someplace."

"How are our finances?"

"Excellent."

"Then that's something, anyway. Suggestions?"

He looked uncomfortable. "I don't know, Vlad. Would it do any good to talk to him?"

"How should I know? We don't know enough about him."

"So that," he said, "ought to be our first step. Find out everything we can."

"If he gives us time," I said.

Kragar nodded.

"We have another problem, boss."

"What's that, Loiosh?"

"I'll bet you're really *horny, now."*

"Oh, shut up."

2

"I'm going to want protection."

When I entered the organization, some three years before, I was working for a guy named Nielar as what we call a "muscle." He controlled a small gambling operation on North Garshos Street. He paid his dues to Welok the Blade.

Welok was a sort of mid-level boss. His area went from Potter's Market Street in the north to Millennial in the south, and from Prance in the west to One-Claw in the east.

All of these areas were pretty tentative and, when I went to work for Nielar, the northern edge, along Potter's, was *very* tentative. The first time I "worked," and the third, were to further the Blade's desire to make this border more certain. His northern neighbor was a peaceable kind of guy named Rolaan, who was trying to negotiate with Welok because he wanted Potter's but didn't want a war. Rolaan became more peaceable after he fell from his third-floor office one day. His lieutenant, Feet Charno, was even more peaceable, so the problem was resolved nicely. I've always suspected Feet of arranging Rolaan's death, because otherwise I can't account for Welok's leaving Charno alone, but I never found out for sure.

That was three years ago. About then I stopped working for Nielar, and went to work for the Blade himself. The Blade's boss was Toronnan, who ran things from the docks in the east to the "Little Deathsgate" area in the west, and from the river in the south to Issola Street in the north.

About a year and a half after Rolaan took the trip to Deathsgate Falls, Welok had a dispute with someone in the Left Hand of the Jhereg. I think the someone was working in the same territory as Welok (our interests don't usually overlap), but I don't know exactly what the problem was. One day Welok just vanished, and his spot was filled by one of his lieutenants—a guy named Tagichatn, whose name I still can't pronounce right.

I'd been working as a troubleshooter for the Blade, but this new guy didn't think much of Easterners. My first day, I walked into his office, a little place on Copper Lane between Garshos and Malak Circle. I explained what I'd been doing for Welok, and asked him if he wanted to be called "lord," or "boss," or if I should try to figure out how to say his name. He said, "Call me God-boss," and we were off.

Inside of a week I loathed him. Inside of a month, another ex-lieutenant of Welok's broke away and started running his own territory right in the middle of Tagichatn's. This was Laris.

Two months of "God-boss" was all I could take. Many of us who worked for him noticed that he made no move against Laris. This was taken as a sign of weakness. Eventually, someone either inside or outside of Tagichatn's organization would make use of this. I don't know what would have happened if he hadn't decided to commit suicide—by stabbing himself in the left eye.

He died late one night. That same night I made contact with Kragar, who'd worked with me for Nielar, and off and on for Welok. Recently, Kragar had been working as a bouncer in a tavern on Pier Street. I said, "I just inherited a piece of property. How would you like to help me hold it?"

He said, "Is it dangerous?"

I said, "Damn right it's dangerous."

He said, "No thanks, Vlad."

I said, "You start at fifty gold a week. If we're still around after two weeks, you get seventy-five plus ten percent of what I make."

He said, "One hundred after two weeks, plus fifteen percent of the gross."

"Seventy-five. Fifteen percent of the net."

"Ninety. Fifteen percent of the net before you split with upstairs."

"Seventy-five. Ten percent before I split."

"Done."

The next morning Tagichatn's secretary came in and found Kragar and me set up in the offices. I said, "You can work for me if you want. Say yes, and you get a ten percent raise. Say no, and you walk out of here alive. Say yes and try to cross me, and I'll feed you to the orcas."

He said no. I said, "See you."

Then I went to an enforcer named Melestav who also hated our ex-boss and who I'd worked with a couple of times. I'd heard he did "work," and I knew he was careful. I said, "The boss wants you to be his personal secretary and bodyguard."

"The boss is nuts."

"I'm the boss."

"I'm in."

I got a map of the city and drew a box around where the dead man's territory had been. Then I drew another box inside the first one. For some reason, in this area of Adrilankha bosses tended to mark the areas by half-streets. That is, instead of saying, "I have Dayland and you have Nebbit," they'd say, "I have up to the west side of Dayland, you have from the east side of Dayland." So the box I drew went from halfway down Pier Street, where Laris's territory ended, to Dayland, Dayland to Glendon, Glendon to Undauntra; Undauntra to Solom; Solom to Lower Kieron Road; and Lower Kieron Road to Pier Street.

I had Melestav get in touch with the other lieutenant and the two button-men who'd worked directly for Tagichatn, and had them meet me a block from Toronnan's offices. When they did, I told them to follow me. I didn't explain anything, I just took them to the office. When we got there, I had them wait just outside and I asked to see the boss.

They let me in while the others waited outside. Toronnan had light hair, cut short and neat. He wore doublet and hose, which isn't usual for a working Jhereg, and every stitch of his gray-and-black outfit was in perfect condition. Also, he was short for a Dragaeran, maybe 6′9″, and of a small build. All in all, he looked like a Lyorn recordsmith. He'd made his reputation with a battle-axe.

I said, "My lord, I am Vladimir Taltos." I took out the map and pointed to the first box. "With your permission, I am now in charge of this area." I pointed to the smaller box within it. "I think I can handle this much. There are gentlemen waiting outside who, I'm sure, would be happy to divide up the rest any way you see fit. I haven't discussed the matter with them." I bowed.

He looked at me, looked at the map, looked at Loiosh (who had been sitting on my shoulder the entire time), and said, "If you can do it, Whiskers, it's yours."

I thanked him and got out, leaving him to explain matters to the rest of them.

I went back to the office, looked over the books, and discovered that we were almost broke. I had about five hundred personally, which can keep a family eating and living comfortably for maybe a year. What I now controlled were four brothels; two gambling halls; two moneylending operations; and one cleaner, or fence, or dealer-in-stolen-merchandise. There were no button-men. (A funny term, that: sometimes it means *full-time enforcer on the payroll*, and sometimes it means *sublieutenant*. I usually mean the latter.) I did, however, have six enforcers working full time. I also knew several enforcers who worked free-lance.

I visited each of my businesses and made them the same

offer: I put a purse with fifty gold in it on the table and said, "I'm your new boss. This is a bonus, or a good-bye gift. Take your pick. If you take it as a bonus and try to mess with me, make a list of your mourn-singers, because you'll need them."

Now doing this left me with damn little cash. They all stayed, and I held my breath. When Endweek showed up, no one except Nielar, who was now in my territory, came by. I think they were waiting to see what I did. At this point, I didn't have enough money to pay for independent muscle, and I was afraid to use an enforcer (what if he wouldn't do it?), so I walked down to the operation nearest my office, a brothel, and found the manager. Before he could say anything, I pinned the right side of his cloak to the wall with a throwing knife, about knee level. I did the same with his left side. I put a shuriken into the wall next to each ear, close enough to cut. Then Loiosh went after him and raked his claws down the guy's face. I went up and hit him just below his sternum, then kneed him in the face when he doubled over. He began to understand that I wasn't happy.

I said, "You've got one minute, by the Imperial Clock, to put my money in my hand. When you've done that, Kragar is going over your books; then he's going to talk to every tag here and find out how much action you've had. If I am one copper short, you are a dead man."

He left his cloak in the wall and got the money. While he did this, I reached Kragar psionically and had him come down. When I had the purse, we waited for Kragar.

The guy said, "Look, boss, I was on my way over—"

"Shut your face or I'll tear out your windpipe and make you eat it."

He shut. When Kragar arrived I went back to my office. Kragar returned about two hours later, and we found out that the books balanced. He had ten tags working, four men and six women, usually taking five clients a day, at three Imperials per. The tags earned four gold a day. Meals came to about nine silver orbs, or call it half a gold a day. He had an enforcer there full time who was paid eight Imperials a day. Miscellaneous expenses were allotted another Imperial.

Each tag took one day a week off, so the place should be taking in 135 gold a day, on the average. The expenses were 51 a day, so the daily profit should average in the mid-80s. Five days to the week (in the East a week is seven days; I'm not sure why) should give about 425 gold a week, of which the manager keeps 25 percent—a little over a hundred. That meant that I should see 320-some gold every week. I had 328, some silver, and some copper. I was satisfied.

I was even more satisfied when, over the next hour, the rest of them showed up with their various takes for the week. They all said something like, "Sorry, boss, I got delayed."

I responded with something like, "Don't get delayed any more."

By the end of the day, I had collected more than 2,500 Imperials. Of course, I had to pay Kragar, my secretary, and the enforcers with that; but it still left me with more than 2,000, half of which I sent on to Toronnan, half of which I could keep.

I was not at all displeased by this. For an Easterner kid who used to work his ass off running a restaurant that earned eight gold in a good week, a thousand plus wasn't bad. I wondered why I hadn't gotten into this end sooner.

The only other major thing I did for the next few months was buy a small narcotics and psychedelics business to give me a cover for my life-style. I hired a bookkeeper to make everything look good. I also hired a few more enforcers because I wanted to be ready for any possible trouble from my managers or from punks trying to muscle in.

Mostly what I had them do was what I call "hang-around duty." This involves just what it says—hanging around the neighborhood. The reason for doing this was that this neighborhood was very popular with young toughs, mostly of the House of the Orca, who'd wander through and harass people. Most of these kids were broke most of the time, when they weren't mugging the Teckla who made up the majority of the citizenry. They came here because it was close to the docks and because Teckla lived here. "Hang-around" duty meant finding these jerks and booting them the Phoenix out of there.

When I was growing up, and collecting lumps from guys who'd go out "whisker-cutting," most of them were Orcas. Because of this, I gave my enforcers very explicit instructions about what to do to anyone they caught a second time. And, because these instructions were carried out, in less than three weeks my area was one of the safest in Adrilankha after dark. We started spreading rumors, too—you know, the virgin with the bag of gold at midnight—and it got so I almost believed them myself.

By my figuring, the increase in business paid for the extra enforcers in four months.

During that period, I "worked" a few times to increase my cash supply and to show the world that I could still do it. But, as I said, nothing much happened that concerns us now.

And then my good neighbor, Laris, showed me why I hadn't gotten into this end sooner.

The day after I'd tried to break up the game and ended by throwing up on the street, I sent Kragar to find people who worked with or knew Laris. I killed time around the office, throwing knives and swapping jokes with my secretary. ("How many Easterners does it take to sharpen a sword? Four: one to hold the sword and three to move the grindstone.")

Kragar came back just before noon.

"What did you find out?"

He opened a little notebook and scanned through it.

"Laris," he said, "started out as a collector for a moneylender in Dragaera City. He spent thirty or forty years at it, then made some connections and began his own business. While he was collecting he also 'worked' once or twice, as part of the job.

"He stayed a moneylender and made a good living at it for about sixty years, until Adron's Disaster and the Interregnum. He dropped out of sight then, like everyone else, and showed up in Adrilankha about a hundred and fifty years ago selling Jhereg titles to Easterners."

I interrupted. "Could he have been the one—"

"I don't know, Vlad. It occurred to me, too—about your father—but I couldn't find out."

"It doesn't matter. Go on."

"Okay. About fifty years ago he went to work for Welok as an enforcer. It looks like he 'worked' a few more times, then started running a small area directly under Welok, twenty years ago, when Welok took over from K'tang the Hook. When the Blade took the trip—"

"From there I know it."

"Okay. So now what?"

I thought this over. "He hasn't had any real setbacks, has he?"

"No."

"He's also never been in charge of a war."

"That isn't quite true, Vlad. I was told that he pretty much ran the fight against the Hook by himself, which was why Welok turned the area over to him."

"But if he was only an enforcer then—"

"I don't know," said Kragar. "I get the feeling that there was more to it than that, but I'm not sure just what it is."

"Hmmmm. Could he have been running another area during that time? Behind the scenes, or something?"

"Maybe. Or he might have had some kind of club over Welok's head."

"That," I said, "I find hard to believe. The Blade was one tough son-of-a-bitch."

Kragar shrugged. "One story I heard is that Laris offered him the Hook's area, if he could run it. I tried to verify that, but no one else had heard of it."

"Where did *you* hear it?"

"A free-lance enforcer who worked for Laris during the war. A guy named Ishtvan."

"*Ishtvan?* An Easterner?"

"No, just a guy with an Eastern name. Like Mario."

"If he's like Mario, I want him!"

"You know what I mean."

"Yeah. Okay, send a messenger to Laris. Tell him I'd like to get together with him."

"He's going to want to know where."

"Right. Find out if there's a good restaurant that he owns, and make it there. Say, noon tomorrow."

"Check."

"And send a couple of enforcers in here. I'm going to want protection."

"Right."

"Get going."

He got.

"Hey, boss. What's this about 'protection'?"

"What about it?"

"You got me, don'tcha? What'd ya need those other clowns for?"

"Peace of mind. Go to sleep."

One of the enforcers who'd been with me from the time when I took over the area was called N'aal the Healer. He got the name first, the story goes, when he was sent to collect on a late payment from a Chreotha noble. He and his partner went to the guy's flat and clapped at the door. They asked for the money, and the guy snorted and said, "For what?"

N'aal came up with a hammer. "I'm a healer," he said. "I see you got a whole head. I can heal that for you." The Chreotha got the message, and N'aal got the gold. His partner spread the story around and the name stuck.

Anyway, N'aal the Healer walked in about two hours after I'd told Kragar to send the messenger. I inquired as to his business.

"Kragar had me deliver a message," he said.

"Oh. Did you get an answer?"

"Yeah. I saw one of Laris's people and delivered it. Word came back that it was fine with him."

"Good. Now, if Kragar would just show up, I could find out where—"

"I'm right here, boss."

"Eh? Oh. Jerk. Get lost, N'aal."

"Where am I?" he said, as he headed out the door. Kragar flipped it shut with his foot and stretched out.

"Where is it set up for?" I asked him.

"A place called 'The Terrace.' Good place. You won't get out for less than a gold apiece."

"I can stand it," I said.

"They make a mean pepper sausage, boss."

"Now, how would you know that?"

"I hit their garbage dump once in a while."

Ask a stupid question. . . .

"Okay," I continued to Kragar, "Did you arrange protection for me?"

He nodded. "Two. Varg and Temek."

"They'll do."

"Also, I'll be there. Just sort of being quiet and hanging around. I doubt he'll even notice me." He smirked.

"Fair enough. Any advice?"

He shook his head. "I'm as new at this as you are."

"Okay. I'll do my best. Any other business?"

"No. Everything's running smooth, as usual."

"May it stay that way," I said, rapping my knuckles on the desk. He looked at me, puzzled.

"An Eastern custom," I explained. "It's supposed to bring good luck."

He still looked puzzled, but didn't say anything.

I took out a dagger and started flipping it.

Varg was of a nastier school than I. He was one of those people who just reek of danger—the kind who would kill you as soon as look at you. He was Kragar's size, which is just a bit short, and had eyes that slanted upward, indicating that there was Dzur blood somewhere in his ancestry. His hair was shorter than most, dark, and worn slicked back. When you spoke with him, he held himself perfectly motionless, making no extraneous gestures of any kind, and he'd stare at you with those narrow, bright blue eyes. His face was without emotion, except when he was beating someone up. Then his face would twist into a Jhereg sneer that was among the best I'd ever seen, and he projected enough hate to make an army of Teckla run the other way.

He had absolutely no sense of humor.

Temek was tall and so thin you could hardly see him if you came at him sideways. He had deep, brown eyes—friendly eyes. He was a weapons master. He could use an axe, a stick, a dagger, a throwing knife, any kind of sword, shuriken, darts, poisons of all types, rope, or even a Verra-be-damned piece of paper. Also, he was a pretty good sorcerer for a Jhereg outside of the Bitch Patrol—the Left Hand. He was the only enforcer I had that I knew, with one hundred percent certainty, had done "work"—because Kragar had given him the job at my orders.

A month before this business with Laris started, a certain Dzurlord had borrowed a large sum from someone who worked for me, and was refusing to pay it back. Now this Dzurlord was what you call "established"; that is, he was considered a hero by the House of the Dzur, and had earned it several times over. He was a wizard (which is like a sorcerer, only more so), and more than just a little bit good with a blade. So he figured that there was nothing we could do if he decided not to pay us. We sent people over to plead with him to be reasonable, but he was rude enough to kill them. This cost me fifteen hundred gold for my half of the revivification on one of them (the moneylender, of course, paid the other half), and five thousand gold to the family of the second, who couldn't be revivified.

Now I did not consider these sums to be trifling. Also, the guy we'd lost had been a friend at one time. All in all, I was irritated. I told Kragar, "I do not want this individual to pollute the world any longer. See that this is attended to."

Kragar told me that he'd hired Temek and paid him thirty-six hundred gold—not unreasonable for a target as formidable as this Dzur was. Well, four days later—four days, mark you, not four weeks—someone stuck a javelin through the back of Lord Hero's head and pinned his face to a wall with it. Also, his left hand was missing.

When the Empire investigated, all they learned was that his hand had been blown off by his own wizard staff exploding, which also accounted for the failure of all his defensive spells. The investigators shrugged and said, "Mario did it." Temek was never even questioned. . . .

So I brought Temek and Varg in the next morning and had them close the door and sit down.

"Gentlemen," I explained, "I am going to a restaurant called 'The Terrace' in a few hours. I am going to have a meal with a certain man and speak to him. There is a chance that he will wish to do me bodily harm. You are to prevent this from happening. Clear?"

"Yes," said Varg.

"No problem, boss," said Temek. "If he tries anything, we'll make pieces out of him."

"Good." This was the kind of talk I liked. "I want an escort there and back, too."

"Yes," said Varg.

"No extra charge," said Temek.

"We leave here fifteen minutes before noon."

"We'll be here," said Temek. He turned to Varg. "Wanna look the place over first?"

"Yes," said Varg.

Temek turned back to me. "If we aren't back on time, boss, my woman lives above Cabron and Sons, and she's got a thing for Easterners."

"That's kind of you," I told him. "Scatter."

He left. Varg dropped his eyes to the floor briefly, which is what he used for a bow, and followed him. When the door had closed, I counted to thirty, slowly, then went past my secretary, and out into the street. I saw their retreating backs.

"Follow them, Loiosh. Make sure they do what they said they were going to."

"Suspicious, aren't you?"

"Not suspicious; paranoid. Go."

He went. I followed his progress for a ways, then went back inside. I sat down in my chair and got out a brace of throwing knives that I keep in my desk. I swiveled left to face the target, and started throwing them.

Thunk. Thunk. Thunk.

3

"This Laris teckla is no teckla."

"Hey, boss! Let me in."

"Coming, Loiosh."

I wandered out of the office, into the shop, and opened the door. Loiosh landed on my shoulder.

"Well?"

"Just like they said, boss. They went in, and I watched through the doorway. Varg stood and looked around; Temek got a glass of water. That's all. They didn't talk to anyone, and it didn't look like they were in psionic communication."

"Okay. Good."

By then I was back in the office. I consulted the Imperial Clock through my link and found that I still had over an hour. It's the waiting that really gets to you in this business.

I leaned back, put my feet up on the desk, and stared at the ceiling. It was made of wooden slats that used to be painted. A preservation spell would have cost about thirty gold, and would have kept the paint fresh for at least twenty years. But "God-boss" hadn't done it. Now the paint, a sick white, was chipping and falling. An Athyra would probably have taken this as a sign. Fortunately I wasn't an Athyra.

Unfortunately, Easterners have always been superstitious fools.

"Boss? Varg and Temek."

"Send them in."

They entered. "Right on time, boss!" said Temek. Varg just looked at me.

"Okay," I said, "let's go."

The three of us left the office, went into the shop. I was heading toward the door when—

"Hold it a minute, boss." I knew that tone of telepathy, so I stopped.

"What is it, Loiosh?"

"Me first."

"Oh? Oh. All right."

I stepped to the side. I was about to tell Varg to open the door when he came up and did it. I noted that. Loiosh flew out.

"All clear, boss."

"Okay."

I nodded. Varg stepped out first, then I, then Temek. We turned left and strolled up Copper Lane. My grandfather, while teaching me Eastern fencing, had warned me against being distracted by shadows. I told him, "Noish-pa, there *are* no shadows near the Empire. The sky is always—"

"I know, Vladimir, I know. Don't be distracted by shadows. Concentrate on the target."

"Yes, Noish-pa."

I don't know why that occurred to me, just then.

We reached Malak Circle and walked around it to the right, then headed up Lower Kieron Road. I was in enemy territory. It looked just like home.

Stipple Road joined Lower Kieron at an angle, coming in from the southwest. Just past this point, on the left, was a low stone building nestled in between a cobbler's shop and an inn. Across the street was a three-story house, divided into six flats.

The low building was set back about forty feet from the street, and there was a terrace with maybe a dozen small tables set up on it. Four of these were occupied. Three of them we ignored, because there were women or kids at them. The fourth, close to the door, had one man, in the black and gray of House Jhereg. He might as well have been wearing a sign saying "ENFORCER."

We noted him and continued. Varg walked inside first. While we waited, Temek glanced around openly, looking like a tourist at the Imperial Palace.

Varg came out and nodded. Loiosh flew in and perched at the back of an unoccupied booth. *"Looks good, boss."*

I entered, and stopped just past the threshold. I wanted to let my eyes adjust to the dim light. I also wanted to turn and bolt back home. Instead, I took a couple of deep breaths and walked in.

As the inviter, it was up to me to select the table. I found one against the back wall. I sat so I could watch the entire room (I noticed a couple more of Laris's people in the process), while Varg and Temek took a table about fifteen feet away. It had an unobstructed view of mine, yet was politely out of earshot.

At precisely noon, a middle-aged (say around a thousand) Jhereg walked into the room. He was of medium height, average girth. His face was nondescript. He wore a medium-heavy blade at his side and a full cloak. There were none of the telltale signs of the assassin about him. I saw no bulges where weapons were likely to be hidden, his eyes didn't move as an assassin's would, he didn't hold himself with the constant readiness that I, or any other assassin, would recognize. Yet—

Yet he had something else. He was one of those rare people who radiates power. His eyes were steady, but cold. His arms were relaxed at his sides, his cloak thrown back. His hands looked perfectly normal, yet I was aware that I feared them.

I was an assassin, trying to be a boss. Laris had maybe "worked" once or twice, but he *was* a boss. He was made to run Jhereg businesses. He would command loyalty, treat his people well, and suck every copper piece possible from everything he had a hand in. If things had worked out differently I might have gone with Laris instead of Tagichatn, and he and I could have done well together. It was a shame.

He slid in across from me, bowing and smiling warmly. "Baronet Taltos," he said. "Thank you for the invitation. I don't get here often enough; it's a good place."

I nodded. "It's my pleasure, my lord. I've heard it highly spoken of. I'm told it's very well-managed."

He smiled at that, knowing that I knew, and bowed his head to acknowledge the compliment. "I'm told you know something of the restaurant business yourself, Baronet."

"Call me Vlad. Yes, a little bit. My father—"

We were interrupted by the waiter. Laris said, "The pepper sausage is particularly good."

"See, boss, I—"

"Shut up, Loiosh."

"So I've heard." I told the waiter, "Two please," and turned back to Laris. "A red wine, I think, my lord. Per—"

"Laris," he corrected.

"Laris. Perhaps a Kaavren?"

"Excellent."

I nodded to the enforcer—excuse me, the "waiter"—who bowed and left. I gave Laris as warm a smile as I could. "This would be a nice kind of place to run," I told him.

"You think so?" he said.

I nodded. "It's quiet, a good, steady clientele—that's the important thing, you know. To have regular customers. This place has been here a long time, hasn't it?"

"Since before the Interregnum, I'm told."

I nodded as if I'd known it all along. "Now some people," I said, "would want to expand this place—you know, add an extension, or another floor—but why? As it is, it brings in a good living. People like it. I'll bet you that if they expanded it, it would be out of business in five years. But some people don't understand that. That's why I admire the owners of this place."

Laris sat and listened to my monologue with a small smile playing at his lips, nodding occasionally. He understood what I was saying. Around the time I finished, the waiter showed up with the wine. He gave it to me to open; I poured some for Laris to approve. He nodded solemnly. I filled his glass, then mine.

He held the glass up to eye level and looked into it, rotating it by the stem. Khaav'n reds are full wines, so I imagine none of the light penetrated. He lowered the glass and looked at me, leaning forward.

"What can I say, Vlad? Some guy's been working for me for a long time. One of the people who helped me organize the area. A good guy. He comes up to me and says, 'Hey, boss, can I start up a game?'

"What am I supposed to tell him, Vlad? I can't say no to a guy like that, can I? But if I put him anywhere in my area, I'll be cutting into the business of other people who've been with me a long time. That's not fair to them. So I looked around a bit. You've only got a couple of games going, and there's plenty of business, so I figure, 'Hey, he'll never even notice.'

"I should have checked with you first, I know. I do apologize."

I nodded. I'm not sure what I expected, but this wasn't it. When I told him that expanding into my area would be a mistake, he came back by claiming that he wasn't doing any such thing—that it was just a one-time favor for someone. Should I believe this? And, if so, should I let him get away with it?

"I understand, Laris. But, if you don't mind my asking, what if it happens again?"

He nodded as if he'd been expecting the question. "When my friend explained to me that you had visited the place and seemed very unhappy about it, I realized what I'd done. I was just trying to word an apology to you when I got your invitation. As for the future—well, Vlad, if it comes up, I promise to speak to you about it before I do anything. I'm sure we'll be able to work something out."

I nodded thoughtfully.

"Goatshit, boss."

"Eh? What do you mean?"

"This Laris teckla is no teckla, boss. He knew what he was doing by moving someone into your area."

"Yeah . . ."

At that point our pepper sausages showed up. Laris—and Loiosh—were right; it was very good. They served it with green rice covered with cheese sauce. They had a sprig of parsley on the side, like an Eastern restaurant does, but they had fried it in butter, lemon juice, and some kind of rednut liqueur—a nice effect. The pepper sausage had the meat of lamb, cow, kethna, and, I think, two different kinds of game birds. It also had black pepper, red pepper, white pepper, and Eastern red pepper (which I thought showed extraordinarily good taste). The thing was hot as Verra's tongue and quite good. The cheese sauce over the rice was too subtle to match the sausage, but it killed the flames nicely. The wine should probably have been stronger, too.

We didn't talk while we ate, so I had more time to consider everything. If I let him have this, what if he wanted more? Go after him then? If I didn't let him have the game, could I stand a war? Maybe I should tell him that I'd go for his idea, just to gain time to prepare, and then come after him when he tried to make another move. But wouldn't that give him time to prepare, too? No, he was probably already prepared.

This last was not a comforting thought.

Laris and I pushed our plates away at the same moment. We studied each other. I saw everything that epitomized a Jhereg boss—smart, gutsy, and completely ruthless. He saw an Easterner—short, short-lived, frail, but also an assassin, and everything that implied. If he wasn't at least a little worried about me, he was a fool.

But still . . .

I suddenly realized that, no matter what I decided, Laris had committed himself to taking over my business. My choices were to fight or concede. I had no interest in conceding. That settled part of it.

But it still didn't tell me what to do. If I allowed that one game to operate, it might give me time to prepare. If I shut it down, I would be showing my own people that I couldn't be played with—that I intended to hold what was mine. Which of those was more important?

"I would think," I said slowly, "that I can stand—more wine? Allow me. That I can stand to have your friend in my area. Say ten percent? Of the total income?"

His eyes widened a bit; then he smiled. "Ten percent, eh? I hadn't thought of that solution." His smile broadened and he slapped the table with his free hand. "All right, Vlad. Done!"

I nodded and raised my glass in salute, then sipped from it. "Excellent. If this works out well, there isn't any reason that we couldn't broaden the experiment, eh?"

"Absolutely!"

"Good. I'll expect the money at my office every Endweek in the first two hours after noon. You do know where my office is, don't you?"

He nodded.

"Good. Naturally, I'll trust your bookkeeping."

"Thank you," he said.

I raised my glass. "To a long and mutually profitable partnership."

He raised his. The edges touched, and there was the ringing sound which denotes fine crystal. I wondered which one of us would be dead in a year. I sipped the dry, full wine, savoring it.

I got behind my desk and collapsed into the chair.

"Kragar, get your ass in here."

"Coming, boss."

"Temek."

"Yeah, boss?"

"Find Narvane, Glowbug, and Wyrn and Miraf'n. Get them here five minutes ago."

"I'm gone." He teleported out, just to be flashy.

"Varg, I want two of them as bodyguards. Which?"

"Wyrn and Miraf'n."

"Good. Now where is—oh. Kragar, go talk to the Bitch Patrol. I want a teleport block around this whole building. A good one."

"Both ways?"

"No. Just to keep people out."

"Okay. What's going on?"

"What the hell do you think is going on?"

"Oh. When?"

"We might have until Endweek."

"Two days?"

"Maybe."

"Vlad, what do you do these things for?"

"Go."

He shuffled out.

It wasn't long before Temek returned with Glowbug. I don't know what Glowbug's real name was, but he had bright, shining blue eyes and a love of the long-handled mace. He was really a pleasant, almost jovial guy, but when he started to come at a customer with that mace, his eyes would light up like some Iorich fanatic's and the customer would decide that, yeah, he could probably find the money somewhere.

It occurs to me that I may be giving you the idea that if you borrow money from me and are thirty seconds late in making a payment, you'll have sixty-five toughs climbing into your windows. No. If we worked like that, it would cost more in free-lance or staff muscle than we'd make, especially with all the potential customers who'd be driven away.

Let me give you an example. About a month and a half before this—eight weeks, I think it was—one of my lenders came in and explained that a guy was into him for fifty gold and wouldn't be able to make his payment. The lender wanted to let it slide, but was that okay with me?

"What's he paying?"

"Five and one," he said, meaning five gold a week principal, plus one gold a week until it was paid off.

"First payment?"

"No. He's made four full, and just the interest for three weeks."

"What happened to him?"

"He runs a tailor shop and hab on Solom. He wanted to

try a new line, and it took a quick fifty to get an exclusive. The line—"

"I know, hasn't taken off yet. What's his business worth?"

"Maybe three or four big."

"Okay," I told the guy. "Give him six weeks free. Tell him if he can't start doing at least the interest after that, he's got a new partner until we're paid off."

So you see, we aren't all that bad. If somebody is really having trouble and trying to pay, we'll work with him. We want his business again, and we don't make a copper by hurting people. But there are always jokers who think it can't happen to them, or bigmouths who want to show how tough they are, or back-alley lawsmiths who talk about going to the Empire. These people kept me in eating money—and then some—for more than three years.

Narvane, who arrived just a few minutes after Temek and Glowbug, was a specialist. He was one of very few sorcerers who worked for our end of the Jhereg, most Jhereg sorcerers being women and staying with the Left Hand. He was quiet, indrawn, and had vaguely Dragon facial features: thin face and high cheekbones, a long, straight nose and very dark eyes and hair. He was called in when a job required dismantling personal protection spells on someone, or clairvoyance, at which I'd match him up against any Dzur wizard I'd met, and even most Athyras.

Three of them leaned against the wall. Temek had his arms folded while he whistled "Hearing About You" off key and stared at the ceiling; Narvane was staring at the floor with his hands clasped in front of him; Glowbug was looking around, as if checking out how defensible the place was. Varg stood away from the wall, not moving, looking like something midway between a statue and a set bomb.

Kragar showed up as the silence was becoming uncomfortable. He said, "The first hour after noon, tomorrow."

"Okay."

Wyrn and Miraf'n came in together. They were already a team when Welok hired them and had remained a team when they started for me. As far as I knew, neither of them had ever done "work," but they had a very good reputation.

Wyrn resembled an Athyra—he had pale blue-gray eyes and always looked like he was on something mind-altering. When he stood, he swayed a bit from side to side like an old tree, his arms hanging limp like drooping branches. His hair was light and shaggy, and he had a way of looking at you, with his head cocked to the side and a dreamy half-smile at the corners of his mouth, that would send chills up and down your spine.

Miraf'n was huge. He was more than eight feet tall, making even Morrolan look short. Unlike most Dragaerans, he had muscles one could actually see. On occasion, he would play stupid and get a big, silly grin on his face, pick up someone he wanted to intimidate, and tell Wyrn, "Betcha I can throw this one farther than I threw the last one. Wanna bet?"

And Wyrn would go, "Put him down, big fella. He was only kidding about testifying against our friend. Weren't you?"

And the guy would agree that yes, it was only a joke, and in poor taste at that, and he was very sorry that he'd bothered the two gentlemen . . .

"Melestav! Come in here a minute, and close the door behind you."

He did, and did. I put my feet up on the desk and scanned the bunch of them.

"Gentlemen," I said, "we're about to get hit. If we're lucky, we have two days to prepare. Starting right now, none of you goes out alone. You're all targets, so get used to it. You'll each be getting orders from me about exactly what you'll be doing, but for now, I just want to let you know that things are starting. You know how it goes—travel in pairs, stay at home as much as you can: the whole deal. And if any of you gets any offers from the other side, I want to hear about it. That isn't just for me, but if you turn them down, you become even more of a target, and I'll want to take that into account. And, by the way, if you don't turn them down, you become much, much more of a target. Remember that—you do not want to fuck with me, gentlemen; I'll destroy you.

"Any questions?"

There was silence for the moment; then Temek said, "What does he have?"

"That's a good question," I said. "Why don't you and Narvane go find out for me?"

"I knew I shouldn't have opened my mouth," he said sadly.

"Oh, yeah," I said. "Another thing—your salaries just doubled. But to pay you, we need to have income. And to have income, we need to keep places open. Laris might go for you, he might go for me, and he might go for my businesses. I'm betting on all three. Any other questions?"

There were none.

"Okay," I said. "One last thing: as of this moment, I am offering five thousand gold for Laris's head. I think you could all use that. I don't expect it'll be easy to collect, and I don't want anybody doing anything stupid and getting himself killed trying for it, but if you see a chance, there's no need to hesitate.

"Wyrn and Miraf'n, stick around the office. The rest of you, that's all. Beat it."

They shuffled out, leaving me alone with Kragar.

"Say, boss—"

"What is it, Kragar?"

"Does that business about doubling salaries apply—"

"No."

He sighed. "I didn't think so. Anyway, what's the plan?"

"First, find four more enforcers. You have until this time tomorrow. Second, we'll see what we learn about what kind of income Laris has and figure out how we can hurt him."

"Okay. Can we afford the extra enforcers?"

"We can afford it—for a while. If things go on too long, we'll have to figure out something else."

"Do you think he'll give us the two days?"

"I don't know. He might—"

Melestav was standing at the door. "I just got a report, boss. Trouble. Nielar's place."

"What kind of trouble?"

"I don't know exactly. I got part of a message, asking

for help, and then the guy got hit."

I stood up and headed out of the office, picking up Wyrn and Miraf'n on the way.

"Boss," said Kragar, "are you sure you ought to go out? That sounds like a—"

"I know. Come along behind me and keep your eyes open."

"Okay."

"Loiosh, stay alert."

"I'm always alert, boss."

4.

"You expect to be unavailable?"

The city of Adrilankha lies along the southern coast of the Dragaeran Empire. It spent most of its existence as a middle-sized port city and became the Imperial capital when Dragaera City became a bubbling sea of chaos, on that day four hundred some years ago when Adron almost usurped the throne.

Adrilankha is as old as the Empire. It had its real beginnings in a spot that recently (in Dragaeran terms) became a cornerstone of the new Imperial Palace. It was there that, thousands of generations ago, Kieron the Conqueror met with the Shamans and told them that they could run wherever they wanted to, but that he and his Army of All Tribes would stand and wait for the "Eastern Devils." From there, he walked alone down a long trail that ended in a high cliff overlooking the sea. It is said by those who make it their business to say things that he stood there, unmoving, for five days (hence the five-day Dragaeran week) awaiting the arrival of the Tribe of the Orca, who had promised reinforcements, as the Eastern army closed in.

The spot was known as "Kieron's Watch" until the Interregnum, when the spells that had kept that part of the cliff from falling into the sea collapsed. I've always thought that amusing.

By the way, for those of you with an interest in history, the Orcas finally arrived, in time. They proved utterly useless as fighters on land, but Kieron won the battle anyway, thus securing the foundations of an Empire of Dragaerans.

Shame about that.

The path he walked is still known as Kieron Road, and leads from the new Imperial Palace down through the heart of the city, past the docks, and finally peters out with no ceremony somewhere in the foothills west of town. At some unspecified point, Kieron Road becomes Lower Kieron Road, and passes through a few not-very-nice neighborhoods. Along one of these stretches is the restaurant my father used to own, where he'd built up the small fortune that he later squandered buying a title in the Jhereg. The result of this is that I'm a citizen of the Empire, so now I can find out what time it is.

When I reached the age of deciding to get paid for what I was doing anyway (beating up Dragaerans), my first boss, Nielar, worked out of a small store on Lower Kieron Road. Supposedly, the store sold narcotics, hallucinogens, and other sorcery supplies. His real business was an almost continuous game of shareba, which he somehow kept forgetting to notify the Empire's tax collectors of. Nielar taught me the system of payoffs to the Phoenix Guards (since most of them are actually Dragons, you can't bribe one about anything important, but they like to gamble as much as anyone, and don't like taxes any more than most), how to make arrangements with the organization, how to hide your income from the Imperial tax collectors, and a hundred other little details.

When I took this area over from Tagichatn, Nielar was suddenly working for me. He was the only one who showed up to pay me the first week I was running the area. Later, he tore out the narcotics business and expanded to running s'yang stones. Then he put in a brothel upstairs. All in all, the place was my biggest single earner. So far as I know, the idea of holding out part of my cut never even occurred to him.

I stood next to Kragar in the burnt-out ruins of the building. Nielar's body lay before me. The fire hadn't killed him; his skull was caved in. Loiosh nuzzled my left ear.

After a long time, I said, "Arrange for ten thousand gold for his widow."

"Should I send someone over to tell her?" Kragar asked.

"No," I sighed, "I'll do it myself."

Some time later, at my office, Kragar said, "Both of his enforcers were in there, too. One may be revivifiable."

"Do it," I said. "And find the other one's family. See that they're well paid."

"Okay. What now?"

"Shit. What now? That cash just about exhausted me. My biggest source of income is gone. If someone delivered Laris's head to me right now, I couldn't pay him. If the revivification fails, and we have to pay that guy's family, that'll do it."

"We'll have more in a couple of days."

"Great. How long will that last?"

He shrugged. I spun my chair and threw a dagger into the target on the wall. "Laris is too Verra-be-damned good, Kragar. He took one shot, before I could move, and crippled me with it. And you know how he could do it? I'll bet he knows every copper I make, where I make it, and how I spend it. I'll bet he has a list of everyone who works for me, strengths and weaknesses. If we get out of this thing, I'm going to build me the best spy network this organization has ever seen. I don't care if I have to keep myself a Verra-be-damned pauper to do it."

Kragar shrugged. "That's *if* we get out of this."

"Yeah."

"Do you think you could get to him yourself, boss?"

"Maybe," I admitted. "Given time. For that, though, I'd have to wait until some of the reports came back. And it'd take me at least a week, more like three, to set it up."

Kragar nodded. "We need to be earning in the meantime."

I thought over a few things. "Well, okay. There's one thing that might work to get some cash. I wanted to hold it in reserve, but it doesn't look like I'm going to be able to."

"What is it, boss?"

I shook my head. "Take charge here. If there's any emergency, get hold of me."

"Okay."

I opened my bottom-left desk drawer and rummaged around until I found a fairly serviceable enchanted dagger. I scratched a rough circle on the floor and made a few marks in it. Then I stepped into the middle.

"Why do you do all that drawing, boss? You don't need to—"

"It helps, Kragar. See you later."

I drew on my link to the Orb and was in the courtyard of Morrolan's Castle, feeling sick. I avoided looking down because the sight of the ground, a mile below, would not have helped at all. I stared straight at the great double doors, some forty yards in front of me, until I no longer felt like throwing up.

I walked up to them. Walking in Morrolan's courtyard feels exactly like walking on flagstone, except your boots don't make any noise, which is disconcerting until you get used to it. The doors swung open when I was about five paces away, and Lady Teldra stood facing me, a warm smile on her face.

"Lord Taltos," she said, "we're delighted to see you, as always. I hope you'll be able to stay with us for at least a few days this time. We see you so seldom."

I bowed to her. "Thank you, Lady. A short mission only, I'm afraid. Where can I find Morrolan?"

"The Lord Morrolan is in his library, my lord. I'm certain he'd be as delighted to see you as the rest of us."

"Thanks," I said. "I can find my own way."

"As you wish, my lord."

It was always like that, with her. And she made you believe all that stuff, too.

As she'd said, I found Morrolan in the library. When I walked in, he was sitting with a book open on the table before him, holding a small glass tube suspended by a piece of thread over a black candle. He looked up as I came in, and set the tube aside.

"That's witchcraft," I told him. "Cut it out. *Easterners* do witchcraft; Dragaerans do sorcery." I sniffed the air. "Besides, you're using basil. You should be using rosemary."

"I was an accomplished witch three hundred years before you were born, Vlad."

I snorted. "You *still* should be using rosemary."

"The text failed to specify," he said. "It's been rather badly burned."

I nodded. "Where were you trying to see?"

"Around the corner," he said. "It was merely an experiment. But please, sit down. What may I help you with?"

I sat in a large, overstuffed chair done in black leather. I found a piece of paper on a table next to it, and a pen. I picked these up and began writing. As I did so, Loiosh flew over to Morrolan's shoulder. Morrolan dutifully scratched his head. Loiosh accepted graciously, and flew back. I handed Morrolan the paper, and he looked at it.

"Three names," he said. "I fail to recognize any of them."

"They're all Jhereg," I said. "Kragar should be able to put you in touch with any of them."

"Why?"

"They're all good at security."

"You wish me to hire an assistant for you?"

"Not exactly. You may want to consider one of these after I'm unavailable."

"You expect to be unavailable?"

"In a manner of speaking. I expect to be dead."

His eyes narrowed. "What?"

"I don't know of any other way to put it. I expect that I'll be dead soon."

"Why?"

"I'm overmatched. Someone's after my territory and I don't intend to let him have it. I think he'll be able to take me, and that means I'll be dead."

Morrolan studied me. "Why will he be able to 'take' you?"

"He has more resources than I do."

"'Resources'?"

"Money."

"Oh. Please enlighten me, Vlad. How much money does something like this take?"

"Eh? Hmmm. I'd say about five thousand gold . . . every week for as long as it lasts."

"I see. And how long is it liable to last?"

"Oh, three or four months is usual. Sometimes six. Nine is a long time, a year is a very long time."

"I see. I presume that this visit is not an underhanded way of soliciting funds."

I pretended surprise. "Morrolan! Of course not! Ask a Dragon to support a Jhereg war? I wouldn't even consider it."

"Good," he said.

"Well, that's all I came by for. I guess I'll be heading back now."

"Yes," he said. "Well, good luck. Perhaps I'll see you again."

"Perhaps," I agreed. I bowed and took my leave. I wandered down the stairs, down the hall, and to the front doors. Lady Teldra smiled as I walked past her, and said, "Excuse me, Lord Taltos."

I stopped and turned. "Yes?"

"I believe you are forgetting something."

She was holding out a large purse. I smiled. "Why, yes, thank you. I wouldn't want to have forgotten that."

"I hope we see you again soon, my lord."

"I almost think you will, Lady Teldra," I said. I bowed to her, and returned to the courtyard to teleport.

I arrived on the street outside of the office and hurried in. When I got into the office itself I yelled for Kragar.

Then I dumped the gold onto my desk and quickly counted it.

"Sacred shit, Vlad! What did you do, lighten the Dragon treasury?"

"Only a part of it, my friend," I said as I finished the counting. "Say about twenty thousand worth."

He shook his head. "I don't know how you did it, boss, but I like it. Believe me, I like it."

"Good. Help me figure out how to spend it."

That evening, Kragar made contact with seven free-lance enforcers and persuaded five of them to come to work for me for the duration. While he was doing that, I reached Temek.

"What is it, boss? We're just getting start—"

"I don't care. What do you have, so far?"

"Huh? Not much of anything."

"Forget the 'not much.' Do you have even one place? Or one name?"

"Well, there's a real popular brothel on Silversmith and Pier."

"Where exactly?"

"Northwest corner, above the Jungle Hawk Inn."

"Does he own the inn, too?"

"Don't know."

"Okay. Thanks. Keep at it."

When Kragar checked in, to report procuring number two, I said, *"Take a break for a while. Get hold of Narvane. Have him stop what he's doing—he's helping Temek—long enough to wipe out the second floor of the Jungle Hawk Inn on Silversmith and Pier. Just the second floor. Got it?"*

"Got it boss! Looks like we're off!"

"You bet your bonus we're off. Get busy."

I took a piece of paper and began scratching out some notes. Let me see, to protect each of my businesses against direct sorcerous attack for two months would cost . . . hmm. Make it one month then. Yes. That would leave me enough to work with. Good. Now, I'd want to—

"Cut it out, boss."
"Huh? Cut what out, Loiosh?"
"You're whistling."
"Sorry."

Burning down an enemy's business is not a normal thing for a Jhereg war. It's expensive and it gets noticed, neither of which is good. But Laris had hoped to take me out with one good shot. My response was to let him see that I was not only not down, but I wasn't even hurting. This was a lie, but it should discourage any more of the heavy-handed nonsense.

Narvane reported in the next morning to say that the job had gone fine. He got a nice bonus for his trouble, and orders to lie low for a while. I met with the new enforcers and assigned them to their tasks, all of which involved defensive work—protecting this or that place. I still didn't have enough information on Laris's operation to know how I could hurt him, so I had to protect myself.

The morning went by quietly enough. I imagine Laris was assessing his position based on the events of last night. He might even be regretting the whole thing—but of course, he was now in too deep to back out.

I wondered how he'd hit me next.

A sorceress arrived promptly an hour after noon. I put five hundred gold into her hand. She walked out onto the street, raised her hands, concentrated for a moment, nodded, and left. Five hundred gold for five seconds' work. It was enough to make me regret my profession. Almost.

An hour or so later, I went out, with Wyrn and Miraf'n as bodyguards, and visited each of my businesses. No one even seemed to notice me. Good. I hoped the quiet would last long enough for Temek to collect a reasonable amount of information. It was frustrating, operating blind like that.

The rest of the day passed nervously, but with nothing happening. Ditto for the next day, except that various sorcerers from the Bitch Patrol came by each of my places and protected them from sorcery. Direct sorcery, I mean. There's no way to protect them from, say, someone levitating a fifty-gallon canister of kerosene over a building, lighting it, and then dropping it. But the enforcers I'd hired should be able to spot something like that, maybe even in time to do something about it.

To that end, I threw down more gold to keep a sorceress on full-time call. Actually using her would cost extra, but this way I was ready.

Reports from Temek indicated that Laris had taken similar measures. Other than that, Temek seemed to be having little luck. Everyone was being very close-mouthed. I had Miraf'n bring him a bag with a thousand Imperials to help open a few of those mouths.

The next day, Endweek, was much like the last, until shortly after noon. I was just hearing the news that the enforcer who'd been killed trying to protect Nielar had been revivified successfully when—

"Boss!"

"What is it, Temek?"

"Boss, you know the moneylender who works out of North Garshos?"

"Yeah."

"They got him, while he was on his way over to you. Dead. It looks like an axe job; half of his head is missing. I'm bringing the money in."

"Shit."

"Right, boss."

I told Kragar, while cursing myself for six kinds of a fool. It had just never occurred to me that Laris would go after the people making deliveries. Of course he knew when they were made, and from where, but it's one of the great unwritten laws of the Jhereg that we don't steal from each other. I mean, it has never happened, and I'll bet you all kinds of things that it never will.

But that didn't mean that those managers were safe. There wasn't any reason in the world why they couldn't be nailed, and the gold simply left on them.

I was just getting up a good round of cursing when I

realized that there were more productive things to do. I didn't know any of these managers well enough to make contact with them psionically, but—

"Kragar! Melestav! Wyrn! Miraf'n! In here, quick! I'm going to lock the doors and sit tight. Divide up the businesses, teleport over to them *right now*, and don't let anyone leave who hasn't yet. Later, I'll arrange protection for them. Now, go!"

"Uh, boss—"

"What is it, Melestav?"

"I can't teleport."

"Damn. Okay. Kragar, cover for him, too."

"Check, boss."

There was a rush of displaced air that made my ears pop, and Melestav and I were alone. We looked at each other.

"I guess I still have a lot to learn about this business, eh?"

He gave me a faint smile. "I guess so, boss."

They reached all but one in time. He, too, was left for dead, but was revivifiable. The gold he was carrying almost paid for his revivification.

I wasted no more time. I got in touch with Wyrn and Miraf'n and told them to return at once. They did so.

"Sit down. Okay. This bag contains three thousand gold Imperials. I want you two to figure out where they're planning to take out H'noc—he runs the brothel that's just up the street. Find out where the assassin is, and get him. I don't know if you two have ever 'worked' before, and I don't care. I think you're up to this; if you don't, tell me. There's probably only one of them. If there's more, just get one. You can use H'noc as a decoy if you want, but you only have about another hour until we're past our usual delivery time. After that, they'll probably be suspicious. Do you want the job?"

They looked at each other, and, I imagine, spoke about it psionically. Wyrn turned back to me and nodded. I passed the bag over.

"Go do it, then."

They stood up and teleported out. About then I noticed that Kragar had come in. "Well?" I asked.

"I went ahead and arranged for them to bring in the gold over the next two days, except for Tarn, who can teleport. He should be in any time."

"Okay. We're broke again."

"What?"

I explained what I'd done. He looked doubtful, then nodded. "I guess you're right, it's the best thing to do. But we're hurting, Vlad. Are you going to be able to get more where we got that?"

"I don't know."

He shook his head. "We're learning too slow. He's staying ahead of us. We can't keep this up."

"By Barlen's scales, I know it! But what should we do?"

He looked away. He didn't have any better idea than I did.

"Don't sweat it, boss," said Loiosh. *"You'll think of something."*

I was pleased someone was feeling optimistic.

5

"For an assassin, you're a real sweetheart."

Here's a dismal thought for you: it seems that every friend I have almost killed me once. Morrolan, for example. I'd hardly been running my area for three weeks when he decided to hire me for a job. Now, I don't work for people outside of the organization. I mean, why should I? Are they going to back me up if I get caught? Can I count on them to pay my legal fees, bribe or threaten witnesses, and, above all, keep their mouths shut? Not a chance.

But Morrolan wanted me for something, and he found such a unique way of hiring me that I was filled with admiration. I expressed my admiration in such glowing terms that he nearly took my head off with Blackwand, the infantry battalion disguised as a Morganti sword.

But these things pass. Eventually, Morrolan and I became good friends. Good enough, in fact, that he, a Dragonlord, had given me a loan to carry on a Jhereg war. But were we good enough friends that he'd do so twice in three days?

Probably not.

It's been my experience that, just when things look bleakest, they continue to look bleak.

"I guess this is my day for dismal thoughts, Loiosh."

"Check, boss."

I teleported from my apartment to a spot just outside of the office building, and went inside without waiting for my stomach to settle. Wyrn was already standing in the street waiting for me, and Miraf'n was by the door.

"How did it go?" I asked.

"Done," said Wyrn.

"Okay. After this, you two might want to make yourselves scarce for a couple of days."

Miraf'n nodded; Wyrn shrugged. The three of us went into the shop, and past it into the suite of offices.

"Good morning, Melestav. Is Kragar in yet?"

"I didn't see him. But you know Kragar."

"Yeah. Kragar!"

I went into my office and found that there were no messages waiting for me. That meant no new disasters, anyway.

"Uh, boss?"

"Wha—? Good morning, Kragar. Nothing new, I see."

"Right."

"Anything from Temek?"

"Narvane is back working with him. That's all."

"Okay. I—"

"Boss!"

"Temek! We were just discussing you. You have something?"

"Not exactly. But listen: I was doing some snooping around Potter's Market and Stipple Road, and stopped in this little klava hole to listen to the gossip, and this old Teckla comes up to me, some guy I'd never seen before, right? And he says, 'Tell your boss that Kiera has something for him. She'll meet him in the back room of the Blue Flame in one hour. Tell him that.'

"He got up and walked out. I followed him, not ten steps behind, but he was gone when I stepped outside. Anyway that's it. I think it may be a setup, boss, but—"

"When did it happen?"

"About two minutes ago. I looked for the guy, then got in touch with you."

"Okay. Thanks. Get back to work."

I folded my hands and thought about it.

"What was it, Vlad?"

I related the conversation to him. He said, "Kiera? Do you think he meant Kiera the Thief?"

I nodded.

"It must be a setup, Vlad. Why would—"

"Kiera and I have been friends for a long time, Kragar."

He looked startled. "I didn't know that."

"Good. Then chances are, Laris doesn't. And that means this is probably straight."

"I'd be careful, Vlad."

"I intend to be. Can you get some people over there, right now, to look it over? And have a teleport block set to keep everyone out?"

"Sure. Where did you say?"

"The Blue Flame. It's on—"

"I know. Hmmm. You 'worked' there about a year and a half ago, didn't you?"

"How the hell did you hear about that?"

He gave me an inscrutable smile. "There's something else," he said.

"Yeah?"

"The owner is into us for a hundred and fifty. I'll bet he's going to be real cooperative, if we approach him right."

"I wonder if Kiera knew that?"

"Could be, boss. She, as they say, gets around."

"Yeah. Okay. We've got about fifty minutes. Get to work."

He left. I chewed on my thumb for a moment.

"Well, Loiosh, what do you think?"

"I think it's straight, boss."

"Why?"

"Just a feeling."

"Hmmm. Well, since it's your job to have feelings, I

guess I'll go with it. But if you're wrong, and they kill me, I'm going to be very disappointed in you."

"I'll bear that in mind."

Miraf'n stepped outside first, followed by Loiosh, then by Wyrn. I came next, with Varg and Glowbug after me. Loiosh flew in high circles, gradually moving ahead of us.

"All clear, boss."

"Good."

All of this to walk one short block.

When we reached the Blue Flame, which was stuck between a pair of warehouses as if it were trying to hide, Glowbug went in first. He came back, nodded, and Loiosh and Varg went in, with me following. The lighting in the Flame was too dim for my taste, but I could still see well enough. There were four booths against the walls on either side, two tables of four in the middle, and three deuces in between. At a far booth, facing me, was a Jhereg named Shoen, whom Kragar had hired.

Shoen was one of those free-lance types who can do just about anything, and do it well. He was small, maybe six feet six inches, and compact. His hair was slicked back, like Varg's. He ran muscle, hustled a little loan business, did some "cleaning," sometimes ran shareba games—at one time or another he'd done damn near everything. For a while, he even worked as an organization contact in the Imperial Palace. He certainly did "work"—in fact, he was one of the more dependable assassins I knew of. If he weren't so addicted to gambling, or if he were a better gambler, he'd have made enough to retire on years ago. I was very pleased that we had him on our side.

Sitting alone at a deuce on the other side was a young kid (maybe three hundred) named Chimov. He had been in the organization for less than ten years, but had already "worked" at least twice. This is considered good. (I did better, but I'm an Easterner.) His hair was black, straight, and cut neatly at ear level. His face had a sharpness reminiscent of the House of the Hawk. He didn't talk much, which the Jhereg considers very good for someone his age.

All in all, I felt quite well protected as I sauntered into the back room. Wyrn, Miraf'n, and Loiosh checked it out in front of me. The room had one large, long table, ten chairs, and was empty.

I said, "Okay, you two, take off."

Wyrn nodded.

Miraf'n looked doubtful. "You sure, boss?"

"Yes."

They left. I sat down in one of the chairs and waited. The only door into the room was closed, there were no windows, and there was a teleport block around the building. I wondered how Kiera would get in.

Two minutes later I was still wondering, but it was academic.

"Good morning, Vlad."

"Damn," I said. "I would have seen you coming in, but I blinked."

She chuckled, gave me a courtesy, and kissed me warmly. She sat down at my right. Loiosh landed on her shoulder and licked her ear. Kiera scratched under his chin.

"So, what did you want to see me about?"

She reached into her cloak and removed a small pouch. She deftly opened it and gestured. I held out my hand, and a single blue-white crystal fell into it. It was perhaps a third of an inch in diameter. I turned and held it up to a lamp.

"Very nice," I said. "Topaz?"

"Diamond," she said.

I spun back to see if she were joking. She wasn't. I studied it again.

"Natural?"

"Yes."

"Including the color?"

"Yes."

"And the size?"

"Yes."

"Guaranteed?"

"Yes."

"I see." I spent another five minutes or so studying the thing. I'm not a lapidary, but I know something about gems. I could detect no flaws.

"I assume you've appraised her. What's she worth?"

"Open market? Maybe thirty-five thousand if you look around for a buyer. Twenty-eight or thirty on quick sale. A cleaner would give at least fifteen—if he'd touch the deal at all."

I nodded. "I'll give you twenty-six."

She shook her head. I was startled. Kiera and I never bargained. If she offered me something, I gave her the best price I could, and that was that.

But she said, "I'm not selling it. It's yours." Then, "Close your mouth, Vlad; you're creating a draft."

"Kiera, I . . ."

"You're welcome."

"But *why?*"

"What a question! I've just handed you a fortune, and you want to know why?"

"Yeah. Shut up, boss." Loiosh licked her ear.

"You're welcome, too," she said.

It suddenly occurred to me, looking at the stone, that I'd seen either her, or her cousins, before. I looked at Kiera. "Where did you get this?" I asked.

"Why in the world would you want to know that?"

"Tell me, please."

She shrugged. "I had occasion to visit Dzur Mountain recently."

I sighed. That's what I'd thought. I shook my head and held the stone out to her. "I can't. Sethra's a friend of mine."

Then Kiera sighed. "Vlad, I swear by the Demon Goddess that you are harder to help than Mario is to sneak up on." I started to speak, but she held up her hand. "Your loyalty to your friend does you credit, but give me—and her—some credit, too. She can't help support a Jhereg war any more than Morrolan can. That didn't stop Morrolan, did it?"

"How did you—?"

She cut me off. "Sethra knows what became of this stone, though she'd never admit it. All right?"

I was struck speechless once more. Before I could talk, Kiera handed me the pouch. I mechanically put the stone into the pouch, the pouch into my cloak. Kiera leaned over and kissed me. "For an assassin," she said, "you're a real sweetheart." Then she was gone.

Later that day, Temek reported in with a list of five establishments owned by Laris. I arranged for some wizards to appear in two of them as customers to begin infiltration. *Wizard,* by the way, can mean either a particular kind of very powerful sorcerer, or, in the Jhereg, someone who does any one specific job very well. If you wonder how to tell which is meant—well, so do I.

Anyway, four of the wizards started penetrating two of Laris's businesses, while Kragar made arrangements for the other places. We hit the first one that evening. Nine toughs, mostly from the House of the Orca and hired for two gold per, descended on the place. Laris had two enforcers there, each of whom got one of our people before he was overpowered. The invaders used knives and clubs on the customers. There were no fatalities, but no one would be wanting to visit that place for a while.

Meanwhile, I hired more of these types to protect my own businesses from similar treatment.

Two days later we hit another one, with excellent results. That evening, Temek reported that Laris had dropped out of sight and was apparently running things from some hidden location.

The next morning Narvane, following up a rumor, found Temek's body in an alley behind the first place we'd hit. He was unrevivifiable.

Three days after that, Varg reported that he'd been approached by one of Laris's people to cooperate in an attempt to get me. Two days later, Shoen found the individual who'd approached Varg, alone. The guy was coming back from his mistress's flat. Shoen finalized him. A week after that, two of the wizards who were infiltrating one of Laris's establishments were blown to pieces in the middle of dinner in a small klava hole, by a spell thrown from the next table.

A week later we pulled another raid on one of Laris's places. This time we hired twenty-five toughs to help us. Laris had built up his defenses, so six of my people took the trip, but they did the job.

Sometime in there, Laris must have lost his temper. He had to have paid through the nose, but he found a sorcerer who could break through my sorcery protection spells. A week after my raid, my cleaner's shop went up in flames, along with the cleaner and most of his merchandise. I doubled the protection everywhere else. Two days later, Narvane and Chimov were caught on their way to escort H'noc in to me with his payment. Chimov was quick and lucky, so he was revivifiable; Narvane was not so quick but much luckier, and managed to teleport to a healer. The assassins escaped.

Eight days later, two things happened on the same evening, at nearly the same moment.

First, a wizard sneaked into a building housing a brothel run by Laris, carefully spread more than forty gallons of kerosene, and lit it. The place burned to the ground. The fires were set in front on the second story and in back on the first; no one was even scorched.

Second, Varg came to see me about something important. Melestav informed me; I told him to send Varg in. As Varg opened the door, Melestav noticed something—he still doesn't know what—and yelled for him to stop. He didn't, so Melestav put a dagger into his back and Varg fell at my feet. We checked, and found that it wasn't Varg at all. I gave Melestav a bonus, then went into my office, shut the door, and shook.

Two days later, Laris's people staged a full-scale raid on my office, complete with burning out the shop. We held them off without losing anyone permanently, but the cost was heavy.

Narvane, who'd taken over from Temek, found one more

source of Laris's income. Four days after the raid on me, we hit it—beat up some customers, hurt some of his protection people, and set fire to the place.

By which time certain parties had had enough of the whole thing.

That day, I was standing in the rubble in front of my office, trying to decide if I needed a new place. Wyrn, Miraf'n, Glowbug, and Chimov surrounded me. Kragar and Melestav were there, too. Glowbug said, "Trouble, boss."

Miraf'n immediately stepped in front of me, but I had time to catch sight of four Jhereg walking toward the ruined building. It appeared that there was someone in the middle, but I couldn't be sure.

They reached the place and the four of them stood facing my bodyguards. Then a voice I recognized called out from among them, "Taltos!"

I swallowed, and stepped forward. I bowed. "Greetings, Lord Toronnan."

"They stay. You come."

"Come, Lord Toronnan? Where—"

"Shut up."

"Yes, my lord." *One of these days, bastard, I'm going to do you.*

He turned and I began following. He looked back and said, "No. That thing stays, too." It took me a moment to figure out what he was saying, then: *"Get ready, Kragar."*

"Ready, boss."

Out loud, I said, "No. The jhereg stays with me."

His eyes narrowed and we matched stares. Then he said, "All right."

I relaxed. We went north to Malak Circle, then headed east on Pier Street. Eventually we came to what had once been an inn, but was now empty, and went inside. Two of his people stopped by the door. Another was waiting inside. He carried a sorcery staff. We stood before him, and Toronnan said, "Do it."

There was a twisting in my bowels, and I found myself with Toronnan and two of his bodyguards in an area I recognized as Northwest Adrilankha. We were in the hills, where the houses were damn near castles. About twenty yards in front of us was the entrance to a pure white one, the great double doors inlaid with gold. A real pretty place.

"Inside," said Toronnan.

We walked up the steps. A manservant opened the door. Two Jhereg were just inside, their gray cloaks looking new and well cut. One of them nodded at Toronnan's enforcers and said, "They can wait here."

My boss nodded. We proceeded inward. The hall was bigger than the apartment I'd lived in after selling the restaurant. The room it emptied into, like a sewer into a cesspool, was bigger than the apartment I was living in. I saw more gold invested in knickknacks around the place than I'd earned in the last year. None of this went very far to improve my mood. In fact, by the time we were ushered into a small sitting room, I was beginning to feel more belligerent than frightened. Sitting there with Toronnan for more than ten minutes, waiting, didn't help either.

Then this guy walked in, dressed in the usual black and gray, with bits of gold lacing around the edges. His hair was graying. He looked old, maybe two thousand, but hale. He wasn't fat—Dragaerans don't get fat—but he seemed well-fed. His nose was small and flat; his eyes, deep and pale blue. He addressed Toronnan in a low, full, harsh voice: "Is this him?"

Who did he think I was? Mario Greymist? Toronnan only nodded.

"Okay," he said. "Get out."

Toronnan did so. The big shot stood there staring at me. I was supposed to get nervous, I guess. After a while I yawned. He glared.

"You bored?" he asked.

I shrugged. This guy, whoever he was, could snap his fingers and have me killed. But I wasn't about to kiss his ass; my life isn't worth that much.

He pulled a chair out with a foot, sat in it. "So you're a hardcase," he said. "I'm convinced. You've impressed me. Now, you wanna live, or not?"

"I wouldn't mind," I admitted.

"Good. I'm Terion."

I stood and bowed, then sat. I'd heard of him. He was one of the big, big bosses, one of the five who ran the organization in the city of Adrilankha (and Adrilankha had about ninety percent of the business). So I was impressed.

"How may I serve you, lord?"

"Aw, c'mon, boss. Tell him to jump in chaos, stick out your tongue, and spit in his soup. Go ahead."

"You can lay off your attempts to burn down Adrilankha."

"Lord?"

"Can't you hear?"

"I assure you, lord, I have no desire to burn down Adrilankha. Just a small part of it."

He smiled and nodded. Then, with no warning, the smile vanished and his eyes narrowed to slits. He leaned toward me and I felt my blood turn to ice water.

"Don't play around with me, Easterner. If you're going to fight it out with this other teckla—Laris—do it in a way that doesn't bring the whole Empire down on us. I've told him, now I'm telling you. If you don't, I'll settle it myself. Got that?"

I nodded. "Yes, my lord."

"Good. Now get the fuck outta here."

"Yes, lord."

He got up, turned his back on me, and left. I swallowed a couple of times, stood, and walked out of the room. Toronnan was gone, with all of his people. Terion's servant showed me the door. I did my own teleport back to my office. I told Kragar that we were going to have to change our methods.

We didn't have time to do so, however. Terion had been right, but he had acted too late. The Empress had already had enough.

6

"I'm going to take a walk."

When I say "Empress" you probably get an image of this old, stern-looking matron, with iron-gray hair, dressed in gold robes, with the Orb circling her head as she issues edicts and orders affecting the lives of millions of subjects with a casual wave of the sceptre.

Well, the orb *did* circle her head; that part is right. She wore gold, too—but nothing as simple as robes. She would often wear... but, never mind.

Zerika was a young three or four hundred, which is like mid-twenties to a human. Her hair was golden—and if I'd meant "blond" I would have said "blond." Her eyes were the same color, rather like a lyorn's, and deeply set. Her forehead was high, her brows light and almost invisible against very pale skin. (Notwithstanding the rumors, however, she was *not* undead.)

The House of the Phoenix is always the smallest, because they won't consider you a Phoenix unless an actual phoenix is seen to pass overhead at the time of your birth. The

Interregnum had eliminated every Phoenix except Zerika's mother—who died in childbirth.

Zerika was born during the Interregnum. The last Emperor had been a decadent Phoenix, and since this was the seventeenth Cycle, the next Emperor had to be a Phoenix too, since a reborn Phoenix is supposed to follow a decadent Phoenix every seventeen Cycles. So far as I can tell, by the way, a reborn Phoenix is an Emperor of the House of the Phoenix who doesn't become decadent by the end of his reign. Anyway, since Zerika was the only Phoenix living at the time, this meant it had to be Zerika. (All of this business about "what makes a Phoenix" is very strange when combined with aspects of the relationships among Houses—such as genetics. I mean, it seems absurd to have the opinion that most Dragaerans seem to have about cross-breeds, when there is, at the moment, no other way to produce a Phoenix heir except through cross-breeding. I may go into this at some point.)

In any case, at the tender age of one hundred or thereabouts she came to Deathsgate Falls and passed, living, through the Paths of the Dead and so came to the Halls of Judgment. There she took the Orb from the shade of the last Emperor and returned to declare the Interregnum at an end. This was about the time my great-great-great-great-great-great-great-great grandfather was being born.

That business about descending Deathsgate Falls, by the way, is quite impressive. I know, because I've done it myself.

But the point is that this background gave Zerika a certain understanding of the human condition—or at least the Dragaeran condition. She was wise and she was intelligent. She knew that there was nothing to be gained by interfering in a duel between Jhereg. On the other hand, I guess what Laris and I had been doing to each other was too much to ignore.

We woke up the morning after the meeting with Terion to find the streets patrolled by guards in Phoenix livery. Notices were posted explaining that no one was allowed in the streets after nightfall, that no groups of more than four could assemble, that all use of sorcery would be carefully observed and regulated, that all taverns and inns were shut down until further notice. There was also the unspoken statement that no illegal activity of any kind would be tolerated.

It was enough to make me want to move to a better neighborhood.

"Where do we stand, Kragar?"

"We can keep up like this—supporting everything and not earning—for about seven weeks."

"Do you think this will last seven weeks?"

"I don't know. I hope not."

"Yeah. We can't reduce our forces unless Laris does, and we don't have any way of knowing if Laris will. That's the worst part of it—this would be the perfect time to start infiltrating his organization, but we can't because he doesn't have anything running, either."

Kragar shrugged. "We'll just have to sit tight."

"Hmmmm. Maybe. Tell you what: why don't we find a few places he's connected to that are legitimate—you know, like restaurants—and make friends with some of the management types."

"Make friends?"

"Sure. Give them presents."

"Presents?"

"Gold."

"Just give it to them?"

"Yeah. Not ask for anything. Have people hand them money, and say it comes from me."

He looked more puzzled than ever. "What will that do?"

"Well, it works with court advisors, doesn't it? I mean, isn't that the kind of thing the connections do? Just maintain good relationships so that if they need something, people will be well-disposed toward them? Why not try it here? It can't do any harm."

"It costs."

"Screw that. It might work. If they like us, that makes it more likely they'll tell us something. And maybe they can tell us something useful. If not right away, then someday."

"It's worth a try," he admitted.

"Start out with five hundred, and spread it around a bit."

"You're the boss."

"Next: we really should get some idea of when we can open something up. Do you have any guesses at all? Days? Weeks? Months? Years?"

"At least days, maybe weeks. Remember—those guards don't like this any more than we do. They'll be fighting it from their end, and all the merchants who aren't involved are going to be fighting it from *their* end. Also, it goes without saying that all the organization contacts in the Palace will be working on it. I don't think it can last more than a month."

"Will it stop all at once, or gradually disappear?"

"Could be either way, Vlad."

"Hmmph. Well, could we open, say, one game, in a week?"

"They might let us get away with it. But once you open up a game, what happens the first time a customer runs short of cash? We need to have someone to lend him money. And then maybe he gets behind on his payments, so he starts stealing. We need a cleaner. Or—"

"We don't have a cleaner in any case."

"I'm working on that."

"Oh. All right. But yes, I see your point. It's all tied in."

"And there's another thing: whoever opens up is going to be pretty nervous. That means that you should really make personal visits—and that's dangerous."

"Yeah."

"One thing we could do is find a new office. I can still smell the smoke in here."

"We could, but . . . do you know where Laris's office is?"

"I know, but he doesn't go there anymore. We don't know where he is."

"But we know where his office is. Fine. That's where my next office will be."

He looked startled, then shook his head. "Nothing like confidence," he said.

Narvane was in touch with me pretty constantly that week, and was slowly getting a feel for the work. After what had happened to Temek, he was being careful, but we were accumulating a list of places and a few names.

I tried doing a small witchcraft spell on Laris, just to see if there was any point in attacking him that way, but I got nothing. That meant that he was protected against witchcraft—and indicated that he really did know me, since most Dragaerans don't think of the art as anything to bother with.

I had enforcers following those people we knew, trying to get their movements down so we could use this information later. We approached a couple of them with large sums, hoping to find out where Laris was hiding, but we didn't get any takers.

The project to make friends with Laris's people went better, although just as slowly. We got nothing useful, but there were indications that we might in the future. I had some people speak to the Phoenix Guards. We learned from them that they weren't happy about the duty, didn't expect it to last long, and that they were as impatient to start earning their gambling money again as we were to start needing to pay them. I considered the matter.

Six days after Zerika put her foot down, I met with Kragar and Smiley Gilizar. Smiley had been protecting Nielar, and was pretty much recovered from being revivified. He got his name because he smiled almost as much as Varg—that is, not at all.

Varg, however, rarely had any expression. Smiley had a permanent sneer. When he looked like he wanted to bite you in the leg, he was happy. When he got angry, his face became contorted. He had picked up an Eastern weapon called a lepip, which was a heavy metal bar with leather wrapped around it to prevent cuts. When he wasn't doing protection, he did muscle work. He'd started on the docks, collecting for a short-tempered lender called Cerill. When Cerill was fed up with being reasonable, he'd send Smiley, and then send someone else the next day to reason with whatever was left.

So Smiley sat there, scowling at Kragar and me, and I said, "Smiley, our friend H'noc is going to open up his brothel tomorrow evening. He's being protected by Abror and Nephital. I want you to go over to help them out."

He sneered even more, as if it were beneath him.

I knew him well enough to ignore this, however. I continued: "Stay out of the way of our customers, so you don't scare them. And if the guards try to shut the place down, just let them. Can you handle that?"

He snorted, which I took for a yes.

"Okay, be there at the eighth hour. That's all."

He left without a word. Kragar shook his head. "I'm amazed that you can get rid of him that easy, Vlad. You'd think you'd have to do a demon banishment or something."

I shrugged. "He's never 'worked,' as far as I know."

Kragar grunted. "Anyway, we ought to know something by tomorrow. Any word from Narvane?"

"Not much. He's been going slow."

"I suppose. But he should at least be checking to see if Laris is opening something."

I agreed. I got hold of Narvane and gave the necessary orders. Then I sighed. "I hate being in the dark like this. We have a good groundwork for the future, but we still know hardly anything about him."

Kragar nodded, then brightened. "Vlad!"

"Yes?"

"Morrolan!"

"Huh?"

"Aren't you his security consultant? Doesn't he have a spy network?"

"Sure, Kragar. And if you want to find out how many sorcerers Lord Whointheheck of the House of the Dragon has, I could tell you in three minutes, along with their specialties, ages, and tastes in wine. But that doesn't help us."

He got a vacant look, and said, "There ought to be a way to use that..."

"If you think of one, let me know."

"I will."

H'noc reached me late in the evening of the next day.

"Yes?"

"Just wanted to tell you that we haven't been bothered by any guards yet."

"Good. Customers?"

"Maybe two."

"Okay. It's a start. Have you seen anyone who looks like he might be working for Laris?"

"How would I know?"

"All right. Stay in touch."

I looked up at Kragar, who was spending more time in my office than in his own these days. "I just talked to H'noc. No problems; no customers."

He nodded. "If we make it through the night, maybe we should open up a cleaner tomorrow."

"Sure," I said. "Who?"

"I know a few thieves who've been talking about getting into that end."

"In the middle of a war?"

"Maybe."

"All right. Check into it."

"Will do."

Kragar found a cleaner, and we opened up a couple of nights later. At the same time, Narvane found out that Laris wasn't doing much of anything. We began to breathe easier. Soon, we decided, the Phoenix Guards would just disappear, and things would be back to normal.

Normal? Exactly what *was* "normal" at this point?

"Kragar, what happens when the Phoenix Guards disappear?"

"Things go back to...oh. I see what you mean. Well, in the first place, we're back on the defensive. He starts moving in on us, we start trying to find out all we can about him—and by the way, we should have more than just Narvane working on that."

"I know. We will, but—it seems to me that this is our big chance to get ahead."

"Uh . . . *what* is?"

"This. Now. When neither of us can attack the other, but we can get our businesses going again. We should push it as far as we can. Get as much going as possible, to build up some cash, and make as many friends among Laris's people as we can, get Narvane and whoever else we can digging into him—the whole bit."

Kragar thought that over, then nodded. "You're right. We've got the cleaner working, that means we can open up a lender. Three days? Two?"

"Two. We're going to be paying extra bribes, but that shouldn't go on too long."

"Right. And once that's going, we could start one of the small shareba clubs. A week from today, say? If everything goes well?"

"That sounds right."

"Good. And we won't need too much protection at first. Let's put Wyrn and Miraf'n helping Narvane. And maybe Chimov and Glowbug, too. But keep them all on the rotation for bodyguards."

"Not Chimov. I don't want any free-lancer knowing too much about what I know. Make it N'aal. He isn't good at it, but he can learn."

"Okay. I'll talk to them, and let Narvane in on it."

"Good. Are we leaving anything out?"

"Probably, but nothing I can think of."

"Then let's get at it."

"It's going to be nice seeing you do some work again, boss."

"Shut up, Loiosh."

It took Narvane only a couple of days to work the extra help into his organization. The day the lender started, I began to get reports from them, and was impressed. While they still didn't know many of his people—and those they did were right at the bottom—they found out seven establishments that Laris was running. To our surprise, none of them had reopened. Laris was lying low. I didn't know whether to be overjoyed or nervous. But there were still Phoenix Guards all over the place, so we felt safe.

A few days later, I opened up a small shareba game, and the next day a game of s'yang stones and a game of three-copper mud. Our list on Laris grew, but he *still* wasn't doing anything. I wondered what it meant.

"Hey, Kragar."

"Yeah?"

"How many Dzur does it take to sharpen a sword?"

"I dunno."

"Four. One to sharpen it, three to put up enough of a fight to make it worthwhile."

"Oh. Is there some point to that?"

"I think so. I think it has something to do with needing to have opposition in order to act."

"Hmmmm. Is this leading somewhere, or are you just being obscure?"

"I'm going to take a walk. Who's protecting me today?"

"A walk? Are you sure it's safe?"

"Of course not. Who's on duty?"

"Wyrn, Miraf'n, Varg, and Glowbug. What do you mean, a walk?"

"I'm going to visit my businesses. Word will get around that I did so, and that I'm not worried about either Laris or the Empire, customers will relax, and business will pick up. True or not true?"

"You're going to show that you aren't worried by walking around with four bodyguards?"

"True or not true?"

He sighed. "True, I guess."

"Call them in."

He did so.

"Stay here," I told him, "and keep things running."

We walked out of the office, past the ruins of the front of the shop (I didn't dare let anyone close enough to me to let them do repairs), and into the street. There were a pair of Phoenix Guards at the northwest corner of Garshos and Copper Lane. We went that way, Loiosh flying ahead, and I could feel their eyes on me. We went east on Garshos to Dayland, and I was surprised that I didn't see any others. We went to the cleaner's, which was set up in the basement of an inn called The Six Chreotha, which looked like it had been slowly falling to ruin for a few thousand years.

I went in to see the cleaner. He was a cheery-looking guy named Renorr: short, dark, with the curly brown hair and flat features that claimed he had Jhegaala somewhere in his background. His eyes were clear, which proved that he hadn't been in the business long. Cleaning stolen goods is not something one can bribe Imperial guards about, so one must be careful not to let them find out one is doing it. Fences always end up with shifty, frightened eyes.

Renorr bowed and said, "I'm honored to meet you at last, lord."

I nodded.

He gestured outside. "They seem to have left."

"Who? The guards?"

"Yes. There were several near here this morning."

"Hmmm. Well, that's all to the good, then. Maybe they're reducing their forces."

"Yes."

"How's business?"

"Slow, lord. But picking up a bit. I'm just getting started."

"Okay." I smiled at him. "Keep it going."

"Yes, lord."

We walked back out, continued to Glendon, followed it to Copper Lane, and headed back north. As we walked past the Blue Flame I stopped.

"What is it, boss?"

"Those guards, Loiosh. There were two of them on that corner fifteen minutes ago; now they're gone."

"I don't like this . . ."

Glowbug said, "Notice the guards are missing, boss? That's a demon of a coincidence. I don't like it."

"Bide," I told him.

"I think we should get back to the office, boss."

"I don't think—"

"Remember what you said about my 'feelings'? Well, this one is strong. I think we should get back right away."

"Okay, you've talked me into it."

"Back to the office," I told Glowbug. He seemed relieved. Varg made no response whatsoever. Wyrn nodded, his eyes dreamy, and his half-smile didn't change. Miraf'n nodded his great, shaggy head.

We went past the Blue Flame and I started to relax. We reached the corner of Garshos and Copper, and Wyrn and Miraf'n looked down both ways carefully, then nodded. We went past the corner and came into sight of my office. I heard a strange, shuffling sound behind me, a false step, and spun in time to see Varg falling to his knees, a look of shock on his face. With the corner of my eye I saw Glowbug falling.

"Look out, boss!"

For the briefest instant, I couldn't believe it was really happening. I had known all along that my life was in danger, but I hadn't really believed that I, Vlad Taltos, assassin, could be taken out as easily as any Teckla on the street. But Glowbug was down, and I saw the hilt of a dagger protruding from Varg's back. He was still conscious, trying to crawl toward me, his mouth working silently.

Then my reflexes took over, as I realized that I was still alive, and that Wyrn and Miraf'n would be covering me from behind. I reached for my rapier as I tried to spot the knife-thrower, and—

"Behind you, boss!"

I spun, and got a glimpse of Wyrn and Miraf'n backing away as a tall Dragaeran with—wait a minute. *Backing away?* They were. They were watching me closely as they carefully stepped backwards, away from the scene. Meanwhile, a tall Dragaeran was coming at me, slowly and steadily, with a greatsword in her hands.

I changed my mind about the rapier and drew a throwing knife with each hand. I wanted to get at least those two bastards who had sold me out. Loiosh left my shoulder, flying into the face of the assassin before me. That gave me the time I needed to take aim and—

Something told me to dodge, so I did, to my right, as something sharp scraped along the right side of my back. I spun, both daggers flashing, and—

Loiosh screamed psionically as there was a ripping in my left side, from behind. I realized that the assassin with the greatsword had gotten past Loiosh. I felt a coldness, and I became aware that there was a piece of steel actually *inside* of me, among my bones and muscles and organs, and I felt sick. I ignored my desire to turn that way, and found the one who had attacked from behind. She was very short and held a pair of large fighting knives. She was staring straight at me, dispassionately. The sword was taken from my side with a sudden wrenching, and I found myself on my knees. The assassin in front of me struck full forward, one knife cutting across for my throat, the other thrusting for my chest. I tried to force my arms up to parry—

And there was blood flowing from her mouth, and she was falling at my feet. The knife she was slashing with scored a gash across my chest. As she hit the ground, the other blade found a home in my stomach. I heard flapping wings behind me and was pleased that Loiosh was alive, as I waited for the sword-stroke from behind that would finish me.

Instead, I heard a voice that sounded remarkably like Aliera's, crying, "You—you're a Dragon!" And the ringing sound of clashing steel. Somehow, I twisted around as I fell, and saw that it was, indeed, Aliera, wielding a greatsword that was taller than she was, and dueling with the assassin. Watching them was Morrolan himself, fury on his face, Blackwand in his hand. Aliera's blade swung high as the assassin's cut low and Loiosh said, *"Twist!"*

I did, but not in time to prevent the other one, who was still alive, from planting her dagger, to the hilt, in my kidney. There was pain such as I had never felt before, and I screamed. A muscle spasm jerked me to my knees and around and down, flat on my stomach, on the blade that was already there, and I only wanted to die quickly and have it over.

For an instant before I got my wish, my face was a few inches from the other assassin's, blood still streaming from her mouth, her eyes set in a look of grim determination. I suddenly realized that she was an Easterner. That almost hurt more than the rest of it, but then the pain went away, and me with it.

7

"I guess there's just a time for doing dumb things."

Lingering trace of a fading green light, but no eyes to see it with. Memory like a well, awareness like a bucket—but who pulls the rope? It occurred to me that "me" had occurred. Existence without sensation, and the bucket hadn't yet reached the water.

I knew what "sight" was when it came, and I found myself staring into a pair of bright round things that I eventually realized were "eyes." They floated in gray fog and seemed to see me. That must be significant. "Brown" occurred to me, looking at the eyes, at about the same moment that I saw a face fitting around them. Looking at the face, other terms came to mind. "Little girl" was one. "Cute" was another. And "somber."

I wondered if she were human or Dragaeran, and realized that more of me had returned.

She studied me. I wondered what she was seeing. Her mouth opened and sound issued forth. I realized that I'd been hearing the sounds for quite some "time" and had not been aware of it. The sounds were utterly dead, as if in a room that was completely without echo.

"Uncle Vlad?" she said again, but it registered this time.

Two words. "Uncle" and "Vlad." Both had meaning. "Vlad" meant me, and I was delighted with the discovery. "Uncle" had something to do with family, but I wasn't sure exactly what. I thought about the words more, deeming them important. As I did so, a wave of green light seemed to come from all around me, bathing me for a moment, then stopping.

I realized that this, too, had been going on for some time.

Sensations multiplied, and I felt that I had a body again. I blinked, and found it delightful. I licked my lips, and that was nice, too. I turned my attention back to the little girl, who was still watching me closely. She seemed relieved now.

"Uncle Vlad?" she said, like a litany.

Oh, that's right. "Vlad." Me. I was dead. The Easterner, the pain, *Loiosh*. But he'd been alive, so maybe . . .

"Uncle Vlad?"

I shook my head, and tried speaking. "I don't know you," I said, and heard that my voice was strong. She nodded enthusiastically.

"I know," she said. "But Mommy's awful worried about you. Won't you please come back?"

"Come back?" I said. "I don't understand."

"Mommy's been trying to find you."

"She sent you to look for me?"

She shook her head. "She doesn't know I'm here. But she's *really* worried, Uncle Vlad. And so's Uncle 'Rollan. Won't you *please* come back?"

Who could refuse a request like that? "Where am I, then?"

She cocked her head to the side, looking puzzled. Her mouth opened and closed a few times. Then she shook her head again. "I don't know, but just come back, okay?"

"Sure, honey, but how?"

"Follow me," she said.

"Okay." She moved away a few feet, stopped, and looked

back. I found myself moving toward her, but I didn't seem to be walking. I had no sense of how fast we were traveling, or from where to where, but the grayness gradually darkened.

"Who are you?" I asked her as we moved.

"Devera," she said.

"I'm pleased to meet you, Devera."

She turned back to me and giggled, lighting up her face. "We've met before, Uncle Vlad." That triggered some more memories that I couldn't quite place, but—

"Oh, Uncle Vlad?"

"Yes, Devera?"

"When we get back, don't mention to Mommy that you saw me, okay?"

"Okay. Why not? Aren't you supposed to be here?"

"Well, not exactly. You see, I haven't really been born yet. . . ."

Wherever we were became completely black, and I felt suddenly isolated. Then, once more, I was bathed in green light, and I remember no more.

. . . the dzur had scored a long scratch in the jhereg's wing. The jhereg's jaws were going for the dzur's neck, but the dzur nearly had its mouth around the long, snakelike neck of the jhereg. The jhereg was of the normal breed, not one of the nonpoisonous giant ones that dwelt above Deathsgate Falls, yet it was one of the largest I had ever seen, and should be able to give a good fight to. . . . I blinked. The scene hadn't changed. The orange-red sky was right, but I realized that I was inside, on a bed, in fact. I was looking at a painting that filled the ceiling above me. Someone's idea of a joke, no doubt, to have me wake up to that sight. Could I view the painting so that it appeared the jhereg was winning? I could and did. It was a nice painting. I took a deep breath and—*I was alive!*

I turned my head and looked around the room. It was spacious, as far as I was concerned—twenty-two and a half feet in the direction of the bed, maybe fourteen the other way. No windows, but a nice circulation of air. There was a fireplace centered in the wall my feet pointed to, with a cozy little fire crackling away in it and sending occasional sparks into the room. I twisted and saw that a door was centered in the other wall. Black candles were scattered throughout, providing most of the light. Yet there were enough of them to give the room a bright appearance despite the black walls.

Black, black, black. The color of sorcery. Lord Morrolan, Castle Black. Yet, he wouldn't have used black candles unless he were doing witchcraft, and I felt no traces of a spell. Nor would he have a painting like that. So—Dzur Mountain, of course.

I leaned back against the pillow (goose feathers, a luxury!) and slowly set about moving my limbs. I made each one move, and each finger and toe. They responded normally, but it took some effort. I saw my cloak and clothing neatly folded on a stand three feet from my head. I noticed with amusement that whoever had undressed me had left Spellbreaker wrapped around my wrist, which was why I hadn't immediately felt undressed.

I heaved myself to a sitting position. I became aware of a general sense of weakness and pains throughout my body. I welcomed them, as more signs of life, and swung my feet over the edge of the bed.

"Going to say hello, boss?"

I spun, and spotted Loiosh high on top of a tall dresser in the far corner of the room. *"Good morning, or whatever it is. I'm glad you're all right."*

He flew down and landed on my shoulder; licked my ear. *"That goes double for me, boss."*

There was a chamber pot in one corner of the room, which I made a much-needed use of. I dressed slowly, finding several of my more obvious weapons neatly laid out beneath the cloak. Most of the contents of the cloak itself hadn't been disturbed. Dressing was painful. Enough said.

There was a soft clap at the door about the time I finished. "Come in."

Aliera entered. "Good morning, Vlad. How are you feeling?"

"Well enough, all things considered." Morrolan was standing in the doorway behind her. We exchanged nods.

"We would have been here sooner," he said, "but we had to visit another of our patients."

"Oh? Who?"

"The 'lady' who attacked you," said Aliera.

"She's alive?" I swallowed involuntarily. Being killed attempting to do a job is one of the very few things that terminates the agreement between assassin and employer; I'd been hoping that they'd both taken the trip.

"Both of them are," she said. "We revivified them."

"I see." That was different. They had the option of resuming the agreement now, or not. I hoped they chose not to.

"Which reminds me," said Morrolan. "Vlad, I apologize to you. The Easterner should not have been able to attack you. I caused ruptures in several of her internal organs, which should have sent her into shock at once. It did not occur to me to continue watching her."

I nodded. "She's probably a witch," I said. "Witchcraft is good for that." He knew that, of course; I was just needling him. "But it ended up all right. How did things go with the other one?"

"She is a very good fighter," said Aliera. "Remarkably good. We fought for more than a minute, and she wounded me twice."

It was nicely ironic that Aliera, who specialized in sorcery, had dueled blade to blade with the one, while Morrolan, one of the finest blades in the Empire, had used sorcery. But both were far, far above the norm at either, so it really didn't matter.

I nodded. "When was it?"

Aliera said, "We performed the revivification as soon as we had you back. You've slept for two days."

"I don't know how to thank you—or was it Sethra?—for revivifying me."

"It was I," said Aliera, "and no thanks are necessary."

"How hard was it?"

She shook her head. "The most difficult I've ever tried.

I thought we'd lost you. It was quite a task to repair your body, even before the revivification. Then I made four tries before it worked. I slept for half a day afterwards."

It was only then that I remembered the dream I'd had. I started to mention it, but Aliera was continuing.

"I think you should be resting now. Try to stay on your back for at least a day. Also, don't—"

This reminded me of something else, so I interrupted. "Excuse me, Aliera, but—how did you and Morrolan happen to be there?"

". . . Morrolan dragged me along. Ask him."

I turned and let my eyebrows do so.

"Kragar," he said. "He explained that you required immediate assistance, but he didn't know the form. I happened to be with Aliera at the time. It seems we were nearly too late. And, to repeat, I apologize for my sloppiness with the Easterner."

I brushed it aside. "All right. I'll take your advice now, Aliera. I think I'd like to sleep."

"Are you hungry?" she asked.

I checked the relevant part of me, then nodded. "A bit. Perhaps when I wake up."

"All right. I'll speak to Sethra about it. Do you feel any nausea, or would you be up to a full meal?"

"I feel fine," I told her. "Just tired."

"Good."

I bowed to each of them and sat back on the bed as they left.

"You're no more tired than I am, boss."

"True. But I am *sore. Quiet for a minute."*

I reached out for contact with Kragar. It took a while, but eventually he responded.

"Vlad! Welcome back!"

"Thanks. It's nice to be alive again."

"I imagine. Aliera told me you'd taken the trip, but they'd brought you back. I was beginning to worry, though. It's been three days."

"I know. How are Varg and Glowbug?"

"Glowbug is okay; the dagger caught his kidney, but we

got to him in time." He paused. *"Varg didn't make it. The revivification failed."*

I cursed, then asked, *"How's our income?"*

"A trickle."

"Hmph. How about standing funds?"

"Around nine thousand left."

"Okay. Thirty-five hundred each for anyone who brings me Wyrn and Miraf'n."

"Boss, they're going to be protected, you'll never—"

"Fine. Then I won't have to pay anything. But put the word out."

Mental shrug. *"Okay,"* he said. *"Anything else?"*

"Yes. Tighten up. I mean, everybody. No action until I'm back, but I don't want anybody *out alone,* ever. *Got that?"*

"Got it."

"And blow another thousand on bumping up the protection on every place we have. I don't want any more surprises."

"Check. Anything else?"

"Yeah. Thanks."

"You're welcome."

"What tipped you off?"

"I got a message from one of those people we've been trying to cultivate as friends. It seems that the thing was arranged in an upstairs room of his tavern, and he decided to help us out."

"Well I'll be. . . . Give him two hundred."

"I gave him one-fifty already."

"Good. Kragar . . . all the Phoenix Guards disappeared, went away, just about the time I left the office. I can't believe that's a coincidence, and I can't believe they have the Empress helping them out—or the commander of the Phoenix Guards, for that matter. Do you know anything about it?"

"Our contact said that he heard it would be 'taken care of.'"

"Hmmmm. I see. Check up on it, all right?"

"I'll try."

"Good. And do you know who those two were? The ones

who got me? They were damn good. They did half the job anyway, even after Morrolan and Aliera showed up."

There was a pause. *"Boss? You don't know?"*

"What are you talking about? How could I know?"

"Think about it, boss. Two assassins. Female. One Dragaeran, one Easterner. One with a greatsword, one with daggers. How many teams like that are there?"

"Oh . . . I—uh, I'll be talking to you later, Kragar."

"Sure, Vlad."

And the contact was broken.

When you talk about assassins, good ones, the name Mario Greymist has a place by itself. He is the best there is, ever has been, or, as far as I'm concerned, ever could be. But after Mario, there are several names that come to mind, among those few who know such things: the ones who are good, dependable, command high rates, and are feared by anyone thinking of making a powerful enemy within the organization.

Most assassins work alone. I mean, murder is a very private thing. But there are a few teams. One of these teams is on the list I mentioned above. I'd heard of them, and their names have been linked to a score of jobs in the last five years. None of these tales is certain, and most are probably wrong, but still. . . . This team involved a Dragaeran, using a greatsword with all the skill of a Dragonlord, and an Easterner using a dagger. Both were women—and the Right Hand of the Jhereg has very few women. (There's Kiera the Thief, and maybe a few others, but they are a rarity.) This pair of assassins called themselves "The Sword of the Jhereg" and "The Dagger of the Jhereg," and no one knew anything about where they'd come from. It was very hard to get hold of them—usually, if you wanted them, you just put the word out on the streets and hoped they'd hear and be interested.

It should be pointed out that the most I've ever been offered for an assassination is six thousand gold, and these two won't even talk to you for less than eight or nine. It had never occurred to me to send them after Laris, because they'd have wanted at least twenty thousand, and there was no way I could raise that kind of cash without committing everything to the one shot—a stupid thing to do since anyone can fail. (I haven't yet, but I've been lucky.)

I wondered how much I was worth, and where Laris had found the funds. I discovered that I was shaking, which was stupid, since the threat was over. Unless they decided to complete the job. I continued shaking.

"You okay, boss?"

"Not really. Let's take a walk."

I stepped out of the room into the cold, black stone halls of Dzur Mountain. I knew where I was at once. To my right would be the library, where I'd first met Sethra. To my left would be more bedrooms. On impulse, I turned to the left. There were doors on either side of the hall. The hall continued past them. I stopped. Could the assassins be in one of these? Or one in each? I decided to keep walking; there was nothing to be gained by seeing them. I mean, as an assassin, I never had anything to say to my targets; as a target, what was I going to say to my assassins? Plead for my life? Sure. No, there was no point in . . . I discovered that I hadn't moved. I sighed.

"I guess there's just a time for doing dumb things, Loiosh."

I opened the door as quietly as I could and looked inside.

She was awake and looking at me. Her face was calm, her eyes expressionless. No question about it, she was as human as I was. Her eyes moved down to my right hand, which I discovered was gripping a dagger at my belt. She didn't seem to be frightened.

She was sitting up, a blue nightgown showing her pale skin in the dim light of a single set of candles. Her hair was dark brown, almost black. Her eyes were darker yet, a vibrant contrast with the shade of her skin. The nightgown was intended to be modest, but it was also intended for a Dragaeran, so it fell rather low on her. She showed no embarrassment.

Her eyes traveled from the dagger to my face. We studied each other for a time; then I forced my hand to relax, and release its grip on the weapon.

Dammit! *I* was the one who was armed, *she* was the one who was helpless. There was no reason for *me* to be afraid of *her*. I managed to speak.

"Have you a name?" My voice sounded dry, almost cracked.

"Yes," she said, in a soft contralto.

I waited for her to continue. When she showed no signs of doing so, I said, "Will you tell me what it is?"

"No."

I nodded. The Dagger of the Jhereg wished to be called the Dagger of the Jhereg. So be it.

"How did your partner evade Loiosh?" I asked.

"She didn't. I gave her some herbs so she wouldn't be affected by the poison, and she just ignored him."

I waited for Loiosh to make some remark about that; when he didn't, I said, "How much was my head worth to you?"

"You'd be flattered."

She continued looking at me. The candles flickered and did things to her hair, and face, and neck, and the shadows of her breasts against the back wall. I swallowed.

Then she said, "We've returned the payment."

I felt a sense of relief, as if the Imperial Executioner had been handed a stay just as he raised his staff. I felt it show on my face and cursed my weakness.

Her eyes came to rest on Loiosh, then she held out her hand. He hesitated and twitched nervously on my shoulders.

"Boss . . ."

"Up to you, chum."

He flew over to her and wrapped his talons around her wrist. She scratched under his chin, going with the scales.

"The jhereg is beautiful," she said.

"His name is Loiosh."

"I know."

"Oh, of course. You must have found out quite a bit about me."

"Not enough, apparently. How did Morrolan and Aliera find out, by the way?"

"Sorry."

She nodded. "You . . . have a talent for making people underestimate you."

"Thank you very much." I walked into the room and let the door swing shut behind me. With a careful effort to appear casual, I sat at the edge of the bed. "So, what now?"

She shrugged, which was worth coming in just to see. "I don't know. Morrolan and Aliera tried to mind-probe me before. It didn't work, so I don't know what they'll try next. Do you?"

I was startled. "What were they trying to find out?"

"Who hired us."

I laughed. "They could have just asked me. Don't worry. They aren't bad types, for Dragonlords."

She smiled back at me, ironically. "And you'll protect me, right?"

"Sure. Why not? You've given the money back, even though you didn't have to, which is proof that you aren't coming after me again. And we Easterners ought to stick together, don't you think?"

She caught the point of that, and dropped her eyes. "I've never 'worked' on a human before, Vlad. I almost didn't take it, but . . ." She shrugged again. I wondered how I could make her keep doing that.

"I'm glad Aliera is good at revivification," I said.

"I suppose so."

"For both our sakes," I added, because I meant it. She looked at me carefully. There was a moment when time did strange things. If I had thrown my stones right, I could have kissed her then. So I did. Loiosh flew off her arm as our lips met, lightly. It was hardly an intense kiss, but I discovered that I'd closed my eyes. Odd.

She continued looking at me, as if she could read something in my face. Then she said, very deliberately, "My name is Cawti."

I nodded, and our mouths met again. Her arms went around my neck. When we came up for air, I reached up and slid the nightgown over her shoulders and down to her hips. She pulled her arms free and began working at the clasp of my cloak. I decided that this was insane. She would never have a better chance of getting one of my daggers and finishing me. *Verra!* I thought to myself, *I think I've lost it.*

My cloak dropped to the floor, and she helped me take off my jerkin. I paused to remove my boots and stockings, then we fell back together, and the sensation of her small, strong body against mine, her breasts against my chest and her breathing in my ear, my hand on the small of her back, her hand behind my neck—I'd never felt anything like it before, and I wanted to just stay like that, forever, and not take it any further.

My body, however, had its own set of rules, and let me know of them. I began stroking her lower spine. She pulled my head away and kissed me; this time we both meant business. I tasted her tongue, and that was nice too. I heard myself making small moaning sounds as my lips traveled down to her throat, then to the valley between her breasts. I kissed each one, carefully, and went back to her lips. She started fumbling for the catch to my breeches, but I interfered by finding her buttocks with my right hand and crushing her to me again.

We drew back and looked at each other once more. Then we paused long enough to send Loiosh out of the room, because love, like murder, shouldn't have witnesses.

"I'll stay here and clean up the blood."

It is sad but true that there are a strictly limited number of times when waking up with the thought, "Hey, I'm alive!" is really astonishing. I hadn't quite hit the limit yet, so I had the obligatory reaction, followed by, "Dear Verra, I hurt."

My side, where the broadsword had taken me, felt hot and feverish, and the area around my kidney, where my lover had put her dagger into me, itched, burned, and ached. I moaned. Then I became aware of the sound of voices, outside the room and perhaps a bit down the hall.

My arm was around Cawti's shoulder, her head on my chest. I enjoyed the sensation, but I was curious about the voices. Moving as carefully as I could, I succeeded in not waking her up. I dressed carefully, making sure nothing clinked.

Meanwhile, the voices had been growing gradually louder. As soon as I felt dangerous again I opened the door, and identified Aliera's voice, although I still couldn't distinguish the words. The dark stone walls of the hallway greeted me; the air was cold and dank, the hallway high and wide. I thought back to my first visit to Dzur Mountain and shuddered. I turned toward the voices. I identified the other voice as Morrolan's. As I approached, he was speaking.

". . . you say may be true, but that hardly makes it any of our affair."

"Any of our affair? Whose is it then? I—there! You see? You've woken up one of my patients."

"It is just as well," countered Morrolan, nodding to me. "You have *exhausted* all of *my* patience."

I was in a long room, dimly lit and filled with books. There were several chairs nearby, all done in black leather, but they were empty. Morrolan and Aliera stood facing each other. Morrolan's arms were crossed on his chest; Aliera's hands were on her hips. As she turned to me, I saw that her eyes, normally green, had turned blue. This is as much of a danger sign as the stiffening of a dragon's neck tentacles. I found a chair and sat down, to ease the pain a bit. This looked like it was going to be a good one.

Aliera snorted at his comment and turned back. "Ha! It's your own fault if you can't see the obvious. What's the matter, isn't it subtle enough for you?"

"If there was anything to see," he parried, "I would doubtless have seen it long before you."

Aliera pressed the attack. "If you had the sense of honor of a teckla, you'd see it as clearly as I do."

"And had you the eyesight of a teckla, you would be able to see what does and does not concern us."

This forced Aliera into a parry. "How could it not concern us? A Dragon is a Dragon is a Dragon. Only this one happens to be a Jhereg. I want to find out why, and so should you."

Morrolan gestured toward me with his head. "Have you met Vlad's assistant, Kragar? *He's* as much of a Dragon—"

She snorted again. "That snake? He was thrown out of the House, as you well know."

"Perhaps so was—"

"If so," she stopthrust, "we'll find out, and then why."

"Why don't you simply ask her?"

"She'd never tell me, you know that. She won't even admit that she *is* a Dragon, much less—"

Morrolan snorted and tried a fancy maneuver, saying, "You know quite well that your only interest in this is to find someone else to be heir."

"So what? What have my motives to do with—"

"Aliera!" said Morrolan suddenly. "Perhaps we should ask Sethra."

She stopped and cocked her head to the side. "Ye-e-ess. An excellent idea. Why don't we? Perhaps *she* can talk some sense into your head."

He sidestepped that. "Let's go see her, then." He turned to me. "We'll be back shortly."

"Fine," I said. "I'll stay here and clean up the blood."

"What?"

"Never mind."

They vanished. I stood up painfully and made my way back to the Dag—to Cawti's room. Cawti. I let the name roll around in my head. CAW-ti. Cawwww-tiii. Cawti. A good, Eastern name. I started to open the door, stopped, and clapped softly.

"Who is it?" came from inside.

"Your victim," I said.

"Which one?"

"Funny, funny."

"Come in," she said. "At your own risk."

I slipped inside. "Good morning."

"Mmmmmm."

"It occurs to me that you didn't kill me last night."

"Oh, but I did," she said. "Six times. But I lost count and revivified you seven times."

I sat down on the bed next to her. She still hadn't dressed. I ignored the dryness in my mouth. "Oh. I must have forgotten."

"You could have killed me, too, you know." Her voice was suddenly serious.

"Yes," I said slowly. "But you knew I wouldn't. I had no such knowledge of you."

"I'll take your word for that." She laughed lightly. I put her laugh, with her shrug, on the list of things I wanted to make her do more often. The candle sputtered, so I rummaged around until I found a few more, and lit them all with the remaining stub. I returned to the bed and tapped her side lightly. She moved closer to the wall and I lay down. She rested her head on my arm.

There were a few pleasant minutes of silence, then I said, "I overheard an interesting conversation just now."

"Oh?"

"Concerning your partner."

She tensed. "What about her?"

I described the conversation. She pulled away from me, leaning on her arm to watch me as I spoke. Her brows were drawn together as she listened. She looked very beautiful that way, too.

I finished the tale, and said, "*Is* she a Dragonlord?"

Cawti shook her head. "That isn't my secret to tell."

"Okay. You look worried."

She smiled a little and put her head back on my chest. "For an assassin, you're quite sensitive, Lord Taltos."

"In the first place, I'm not an assassin—you've been listening to too many rumors about me. In the second, the same goes for you, doubled. And in the third, isn't 'Lord Taltos' a bit out of place, all things considered?"

She chuckled. "As you wish, Vlad. Vladimir." She repeated it, slowly. "Vladimir. VLA-di-meer. Vlaaaadimeer. Vladimir. I like it. A good Eastern name."

"Shit," I said. "Help me off with this damned jerkin, will you? And careful not to stab yourself. . . ."

Some time later, while engaged in serious snuggling, I said, "Morrolan and Aliera are liable to check up on your partner, you know."

"Mmmmm. They won't find anything."

"Don't be too sure, Cawti. They've surprised me before."

She tsked. "Shouldn't let yourself be surprised, Vladimir."

I snorted, and withheld a few remarks. "I'm serious. They're bound to find out something. You don't have to tell me what it is, but you ought to think about it. Have you been in touch with her?"

"Of course."

"Then warn her—"

"Why do you care?"

"Huh? I don't know. Jhereg are Jhereg, I guess. You aren't a threat to me anymore, and I don't see why they should be meddling. Or Aliera, rather. Morrolan doesn't see why, either."

"Mmmmmm."

I shrugged, causing her head to bounce on my chest. She giggled, which amazed and delighted me no end. Have you ever met an assassin who giggled? The absurdity of the whole situation was—

I decided that I had to get out of there. I sat up, dislodging her. "I'm going to check on our hosts and see what they're doing now."

"Like hell you are, my love. What's really bothering you?"

"What did you call me?"

She sat up too, the bedclothes falling to her waist. She glared. "Don't start getting mushy with me, you murdering Easterner."

"What did you call me?"

"A murdering Easterner."

"Yes, dear, and so are you. I meant before that."

"Vladimir . . ."

"Oh, Deathsgate. I'm getting out of here." I dressed quickly and stepped into the hall, using all of my willpower to avoid looking back at her. I returned to my room, favoring my injured side, and collapsed on the bed. Loiosh gave me a good chewing out (literally) for deserting him, after which I got in touch with Kragar.

"What's new?" I asked him.

"I have some information about the Phoenix Guards—they weren't just withdrawn in the area around where the job was done, they were taken out of the whole area. They're gone."

"Great. Well, I'm pleased they aren't around, but I wonder what it means. Any ideas?"

"No."

"Okay. I want you to try to find out something for me."

"Sure. What?"

"Everything you can on the Sword of the Jhereg."

"Is this a joke?"

"Do you think it's likely to be?"

"Fine. I'll get back to you in a hundred years or so. Vlad, how *am I—"*

"She was once a Dragonlord; that should help. She was probably expelled."

"Wonderful. Should I try to bribe a Lyorn or a Dragon?"

"The Lyorn would be safer, but the Dragon is more likely to help."

"I was being sarcastic."

"I know. I wasn't."

He sighed telepathically. *"I'll see what I can do. Would you mind telling me what we're doing this for?"*

That was a tricky one. I didn't feel like telling him that his boss had become infatuated with his own executioner. *"Oh,"* I told him, *"I'm sure you can figure it out if you really work at it."*

Silence, then: *"You want to find out if there was anything shady in her expulsion, so you can clear her and have her owe you a favor, and then turn her back on Laris. Right? Not bad."*

Hmmmm. Not bad at all. *"Clever,"* I told him. It *was* clever. I'd have to give him a bonus, if it worked out. *"Now, get on it."* I broke the contact. I stretched out on the bed. After all of this, I really *did* need to sleep. I also needed to get my emotions under control.

The first thing I noticed when I woke up was that my side and back didn't hurt so much. Also, I actually felt refreshed. I lay there for a few minutes, just breathing and enjoying it, then forced myself to get up. In addition to feeling refreshed, I also felt filthy from sleeping in my clothes. I stripped and found a tub of water in the corner, did a quick spell to heat it, and washed. As I did this, I managed to put Cawti out of my mind, at least for a little while, and concentrate on my real problem—Laris.

The idea Kragar had had wasn't bad at all, but it depended on too many things that were outside of my control. Still, it was worth checking into. Also worth checking into was the question of why the Phoenix Guards had chosen that moment to leave. How could he have arranged that? Where had the orders come from?

I snapped my fingers, getting soapy water in my eye. *That* question, at least, I could get answered. I concentrated on a certain Tsalmoth, who worked for Morrolan and reported directly to me. . . .

"Who is it?" said Fentor.

"Vlad."

"Oh! Yes, milord?"

"We need some information. . . ." I explained what I was after, and he agreed to check into it. I broke the contact and chatted with Loiosh while I finished up my bath. I looked disgustedly at my filthy clothes, shrugged, and started to put them on again.

"Check the dressing table, boss."

"Eh?"

But I did, then smiled. Aliera had been thorough. I donned the change of clothes happily, then stepped out into the hall with Loiosh riding on my right shoulder. It seemed as if I were beginning to get things done. Good. I wandered down to the library, found it empty, and took the stairs up to where the dining room and various sitting rooms were.

The next thing, I decided, was to see if I could get more information from whoever it was that had tipped Kragar off about the assassination. The fact that we'd actually learned something from him was a very good sign. My biggest problem was still lack of information, and this could mean we were starting to solve it. I thought about getting in touch with Kragar again to ask him to work on that more, but decided against it. As they say: if you have someone stand for you, don't jog his sword arm while he does.

I found Morrolan and Aliera in the first sitting room I came to, along with Sethra. Sethra Lavode: tall, pale, undead, and faintly vampiric. I'd heard her age placed at anything from ten to twenty thousand years, which is a significant portion of the age of the Empire itself. She dressed in and surrounded herself with black, the color of sorcery. She lived in Dzur Mountain; maybe she *was* Dzur Mountain, for there are no records of a time when she, or someone of her family, didn't live there. Dzur Mountain was its own mystery, and not subject to being understood by one such as me. The same may be said of Sethra.

Physically, though, she had the high, thin features of the House of the Dragon. The upward slant of her eyes and the unusually extreme point to her ears made one think of Dzurlords. There had been rumors that she was half Dzur herself, but I doubted them.

To Sethra, even more than to most Dragaerans, an Easterner's lifetime was a blink of an eye. Maybe that's why she was so tolerant of me. (Morrolan's tolerance was due to having lived among Easterners for many years of his youth, during the Interregnum. Aliera's tolerance I've never understood; I suspect she was just being polite to Morrolan.) Most Dragaerans had heard of Sethra Lavode, but few had met her. She was periodically considered a hero, and had been Warlord of the Empire (while she was still living) and Captain of the Lavodes (when there were still Lavodes). At other times, such as the present, she was considered an evil enchantress and Dzurlord bait. Periodically, some fledgling hero would go up the Mountain to destroy her. She turned them into jhegaala or yendi and sent them back. I'd told her that this wasn't going to help, but she just smiled.

At her side was the dagger called Iceflame, which was sort of Dzur Mountain in hand, or something. I don't know enough about it to say more, and thinking about it makes me nervous.

I bowed to each of them, and said, "Thank you for the sanctuary, Sethra."

"It's no trouble, Vlad," she responded. "I enjoy your company. I'm pleased to see that you're recovering."

"So am I." I sat down, then asked, "What can you fine specimens of Dragonhood tell me about the Phoenix Guard?"

Morrolan arched an eyebrow. "What did you wish to know? Is it your desire to join?"

"Could I?"

"I'm afraid," he said, "that your species is against you there."

"But not my House?"

He looked startled and glanced at Aliera.

She said, "A Jhereg could join if he wanted to. There have been some, I think—none who are actually a part of the business end, I suppose, but some who've bought Jhereg titles instead of being Houseless."

I nodded. "So it isn't all Dragons, eh? That's what I was wondering about."

"Oh, no," said Aliera. "It's mostly Dragons, because all Dragons must serve periodically, but there are others from every House in the guards—except Athyra, who are never interested, and Phoenix, because there aren't enough of them."

"Suppose some colonel of some army of Dragonlords is serving. Would he be a colonel in the guards?"

"No," said Sethra. "Rank among the guards has nothing to do with any other rank. Officers in private armies often serve under their own blademen."

"I see. Does this ever cause problems?"

"No," said Aliera.

"Why the interest?" asked Sethra.

"I'm bothered by the fact that the guards who were enforcing the Imperial Edict left just at the right time for our friends to nail me. I can't believe it was coincidence."

They looked at each other. "I can't think of any way," said Sethra.

"Whose decision would it have been? The Empress's? Or whoever leads the guards?"

"The Empress sent them; she would have had to order their withdrawal," said Aliera. Morrolan nodded.

"All right," I said, "I don't think she would have been involved in this on purpose, would she?" Three heads shook. "Then is there anyone who could have made the suggestion to her that 'now would be a good time,' and be confident that she'd act on it at once?"

Sethra and Aliera looked at Morrolan, who was at court

more often than they. He drummed his fingers on the arm of his chair. "Her lover," he said, "is said to be an Easterner. I've never met him, but he might have such influence. Then there are her advisors, but, to be candid, she hardly listens to most of them. I believe that she listens seriously to me, but I could be deluding myself. And, in any case, I made no such request of her. She pays attention to Sethra the Younger, but Sethra has no interest in anything save invasion plans for the East."

Sethra Lavode nodded. "It's good to have an ambition," she said. "Sethra the Younger is the only apprentice I've ever had who's never tried to kill me."

I turned back to Morrolan. "You can't think of anyone else?"

"Not at present."

"All right then, what else? A faked message, maybe? Do this right now, signed so-and-so?"

"Who," said Morrolan, "would write a message rather than reach her psionically?"

"Well, someone she doesn't speak with often. It must be hard to reach her directly, so—"

"No it isn't," said Aliera, looking at me as if puzzled.

"It isn't?"

"Of course not. Any citizen can reach Zerika through his link. Didn't you know that?"

"No . . . but she must get thousands of people—"

"Not really," she said. "If she doesn't consider it worth her time, she destroys the person. This keeps the amount of contact down quite a bit."

"Oh. . . . My father never saw fit to mention that. I guess he was afraid I might do it. In any case, I still don't see who could and would have convinced her to withdraw the troops. Morrolan, you're well respected around court. Will you try to find out for me?"

"No," said Morrolan. "As I have explained to you, I will have nothing to do with any Jhereg war, directly or indirectly."

"Yeah, okay." I was pleased to see Aliera shoot him a brief look of disgust. It occurred to me then that the easiest thing to do would be to create something real that would make the Empress want to pull the troops out. What could it be? Civil disturbance? Threat of an invasion of some sort?

"Kragar."

"Yes, Vlad?"

"See if there was anything going on in the city that would have called for Phoenix Guards to handle."

"Good idea, boss."

"That's what I pay myself for."

Then I reached Fentor and had him check into any possible external threats. With any luck, I'd know within a day or two. I turned my attention back to the others. Aliera and Sethra were deep into another discussion.

"Certainly," Sethra was saying. "And as far as I'm concerned, let her."

Aliera frowned. "We're just getting on our feet, Sethra. We can't afford to go off East with tens of thousands of troops until we're sure the Empire is stable."

"What's this about?" I asked.

"You set off another argument, Vlad," Morrolan explained. "Aliera is opposed to Sethra the Younger's conquering the East until the Empire is stable. Sethra the Younger thinks that will make it stable, and our own Sethra," he indicated her with his head, "feels, as I do, that since Sethra—the other one—wants to do it, why not? What harm is there? They'll throw us out again in a few hundred or a thousand years. That was why Kieron the Conqueror left them there in the first place—so we'd have someone to fight and wouldn't tear ourselves apart."

I could have said many things about this, but I let it go.

"That isn't the point," said Aliera. "If we drain off enough resources, what happens if a *real* enemy shows up? The Easterners are no threat to us now—"

"*What* real enemy?" said Sethra. "There isn't—"

I stood and left them to their argument. It couldn't have anything to do with me, in any case.

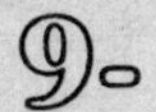

"I guess they wanted to see you."

I returned to my room and decided that I wanted to see Cawti again; also, that I was looking forward to dinner that evening with Sethra, Morrolan, and Aliera. I realized that I could become very comfortable at Dzur Mountain, while Kragar kept things going at the office. In other words, while everything I'd built up went over Deathsgate Falls. Not that Kragar was incompetent, but there are certain things one must do oneself, and I'd been gone four days already.

"Aliera?"

After a pause, a response came. *"Yes, Vlad?"*

"Something has come up. I'm going to have to return to the office right away. Please convey my apologies to Sethra and Morrolan."

"As you wish. But don't exert yourself."

"I wouldn't think of it."

"Would you like help with the teleport?"

"Yes, please. That would be very nice."

"All right, I'll be right down," she concluded vocally, standing in front of me. Damn show-off. I gave her an

image of the alley behind a row of buildings facing Malak Circle, and pulled back to show where it was relative to parts of Adrilankha that she knew. She nodded.

"Ready?" she asked.

"Ready."

There was a twist, and a burbling in my stomach, and I was there. I could have teleported to just outside the office building, but I wanted to look around and get a feel for the area, as well as give my stomach a chance to recover.

Walking through the streets wasn't as risky as it may sound. Though I didn't have any bodyguards, no one even knew that I was around. The only way Laris could really get me was to have an assassin standing around next to my office, hoping I'd walk back in. I'd never taken "work" like that, but I have an idea of the risks associated with it. The longer you stand around a place, the more chance there is that someone will be able to identify you as the one doing the job. Paying someone to do that would cost more than paying the Sword and the Dagger to just finalize the individual. So I wasn't very worried.

The neighborhood looked a bit subdued. It was early afternoon, and this area didn't really get going until nightfall, but it was still too quiet. Have you ever known a part of a city so well that you could tell what kind of mood it was in? So well that the scent of barbecuing lyorn legs told you that all was not normal? So you could hear that the street-hawkers were just a little bit more quiet than usual? That tradesmen and Teckla were wearing clothes with, perhaps, just a bit less color than they normally did? Where the scented fires of a hundred passersby making offerings to a dozen gods at a score of small altars brought a sense of weariness to the heart, instead of renewal?

I knew this part of Adrilankha that well, and that was the kind of mood it was in. I didn't need to talk to Kragar to know that business hadn't recovered. I thought about this, and, as I approached the office itself, I discovered something very important: Laris wasn't worried about money.

"Look out, boss!"

Not again, by the teeth of Dzur Mountain! I hit the

ground, rolled to my right, came up to my knees, and spotted two Jhereg that I didn't recognize moving at me from either side. *Two* of them, for the love of Verra! They both held daggers. Loiosh was in front of one, buffeting his face and trying to sink his teeth into him. The other one suddenly stumbled and fell to his knees a few feet away from me, with three shuriken sticking out of him. I realized then that I'd thrown them. Not bad, Vlad.

I scrambled to my feet and spun, looking for more. I didn't spot them, so I turned back in time to see the other assassin fall to the ground. As he fell, I saw N'aal behind him, holding a large fighting knife with fresh blood on it. Next to him was Chimov, also holding a knife, looking around anxiously.

"Boss!" said N'aal.

"No," I snapped. "I'm Kieron the Conqueror. What's going on around here? Why do we have Verra-be-damned assassins standing outside the Verra-be-damned office in the middle of the Verra-be-damned afternoon?"

Chimov just shrugged. N'aal said, "I guess they were looking for you, boss."

Some days everyone and his sibling is a Verra-be-damned jongleur. I brushed past them and stormed into the office. Melestav jumped when I came in, but relaxed when he saw it was me. Kragar was in my office, sitting in my Verra-be-damned chair. He greeted me warmly.

"Oh, it's you," he said.

One . . . two . . . three . . . four. . . .

"Kragar, may I please have my chair back?"

"Oh, sure, boss. Sorry. Whatsamatter, hard day dodging assassins? I assumed you wanted some excitement, or why did you go walking into the middle of them without letting anyone know you were coming? I mean, it would have been easy—"

"ʃ You're pushing it ʅ."

He got up. "Whatever you say, Vlad."

"Kragar, just what is going on around here?"

"Going on?"

I gestured toward the outside.

"Oh. Nothing."

"Nothing? You mean 'no business'?"

"Almost none."

"But what about those assassins?"

"I didn't know they were there, Vlad. D'you think I'd have just left them there?"

"But they must be costing Laris a fortune."

He nodded. I was interrupted by contact with Melestav.

"Yeah?"

"N'aal is here."

"Send him in."

He came in. "Boss, I—"

"Just a minute. Three things. First, good work taking out the one. Second, next time I'll expect you to spot them before they spot me. Three, next time I'm almost nailed like that, if you're around, keep your bleeding wiseass remarks to yourself or I'll cut your bleeding throat for you. Got it?"

"Yeah, boss. Sorry."

"Okay. What d'you want?"

"I thought you'd want these." He tossed my shuriken, complete with bloodstains, on my desk. "I remember hearing that you don't like them left around, and—"

I stood up, walked around my desk, and slipped a dagger out from my cloak. Before N'aal could react, I put it in him, between the forth and fifth ribs, angled up. A look of shock came into his face as I stepped out of the way. Then he fell.

I turned to Kragar, still gripped by fear and icy rage. Also, my back and side hurt like the Great Sea of Chaos. "Kragar, you are a very fine administrative assistant. But if you ever want to run an area, make it as far from me as possible, or else learn how to keep discipline. That guy's no fool; he should know better than to walk in here with a murder weapon, with the corpse's blood still on it. In the four days I've been gone, you've managed to convince everyone around here that they don't have to think anymore, and as a result I almost got butchered out there. You son-of-a-bitch, this is my *life* we're talking about!"

"Take it easy, boss. Don't—"

"Shut up."

"Now," I continued, "see if you can get him revivified. Out of your pocket. If not, *you* may have the honor of giving his next of kin the bonus. Understand?"

Kragar nodded, looking genuinely crestfallen. "I'm sorry, Vlad," he said, and seemed to be looking for something else to say.

I went back to my desk, sat down, leaned back and shook my head. Kragar wasn't incompetent, at most things. I really *didn't* want to lose him. After this, I should probably do something to show I trusted him. I sighed. "Okay, let's forget it. I'm back now. There's something I want you to do."

"Yeah?"

"N'aal was not completely wrong. I should not have left the shuriken in the body; but he should not have brought them back to me. I don't know that the Empire ever employs witches, but if it does, a witch could trace that weapon back to its wielder."

Kragar listened silently. He knew nothing about witchcraft.

"It has to do with body aura," I explained. "Anything that's been around me for any length of time is going to pick up a sort of psychic 'scent' that a witch can identify."

"So, what do you do about it? You can't count on always taking the weapon with you."

"I know. So what I'm going to do is to start changing weapons every couple of days or so, so that nothing is on me long enough to pick up my aura. I'm going to make a list of all my weapons. I want you to go around and get ones to match. I'll put the ones I'm done with in a box, and you can use them for trade next time, which should cut down on the cost a bit. Okay?"

He looked startled. Well, I wasn't surprised. I was putting a lot of trust in him to tell him what weapons I had concealed about me, even if, as he would suspect, I were keeping a few back. But he nodded.

"Good," I said. "Come back in an hour and I'll have the

list made up. Memorize and destroy it."

"Check, boss."

"Good. Now go away."

"Boss . . ."

"Sorry I snapped at you, Loiosh. And good work with that assassin."

"Thanks, boss. And don't worry about it. I understand."

Loiosh had always been understanding, I decided. It was only then, as I began writing, that it really hit me just how close I'd come once again. I reached the trash bucket just before my stomach emptied itself. I got a glass of water and rinsed out my mouth, then had Melestav empty and clean the bucket. I sat there shaking for some time before I got to work on the list for Kragar.

I gave Kragar the list, and he took off to fill it. Shortly after that I got a message from Melestav.

"Boss . . . there are some people here to see you."

"Who?"

"People in uniform."

"Oh shit. Well, I shouldn't be surprised." I made sure there was nothing incriminating on my desk. *"Okay, send them in."*

"How bad do you suppose this is going to be, Loiosh?"

"You can always claim self-defense, boss."

The door opened and two Dragaerans dressed in the golden uniforms of the House of Phoenix came marching in. One looked around the office contemptuously, as if to say, "So this is how the scum live." The other looked at me with a similar expression, as if to say, "So this is the scum."

"Greetings, my lords," I said. "How may I serve the Empire?"

The one who was looking at me said, "You are Baronet Vlad of Taltos?" He pronounced it "Taltoss," instead of "Taltosh," so he must have had written orders, for whatever that was worth.

"Baronet Taltos will do," I said. "I am at your service, lords."

The other one turned his glance to me, snorted, and said, "I'll bet."

The first one asked me, "What do you know about it?"

"About what, my lord?"

He shot a glance at the other, who closed the door of my office. I took a deep breath, and exhaled slowly, knowing what was coming. Well, it happens sometimes. When the door was shut, the one who'd been doing most of the talking pulled a dagger from his belt.

I swallowed and said, "My lord, I'd like to help—" which was as far as I got before the hilt of the dagger, held in his palm, smashed into the side of my head. I went flying out of the chair and landed in the corner.

"Loiosh, don't do anything."

There was a pause then, *"I know, boss, but—"*

"Nothing!"

"Okay, boss. Hang in there."

The one who'd just hit me was standing over me now. He said, "Two men were murdered just outside of the door of this place, Jhereg." He made it sound like a curse. "What do you know about it?"

"Lord," I said, "I don't know *oomph!*" as his foot took me in the stomach. I'd seen it just in time to move forward, so he missed my solar plexus.

The other one came up then. "Did you hear him, Menthar? He don't know oomph. How about that?" He spat on me. "I think we should take him to the barracks. What do you think?"

Menthar muttered something and kept looking at me. "I've heard you're a tough one, Whiskers. Is that true?"

"No, lord," I told him.

He nodded and said to the other one, "This isn't a Jhereg; this is a Teckla. Look at him squirm. Doesn't it make you sick?"

His partner said, "What about those two murders, Teckla? You sure you don't know anything about them?" He reached down and hauled me up, so that I was against the back wall. "You *real* sure?"

I said, "I don't know what—" and he caught me under the chin with the pommel of his dagger, which had been hidden in his hand. My head cracked against the wall and I felt my jaw break. I must have lost consciousness for an instant, because I don't remember sliding to the floor.

Then Menthar said, "You hold him for me."

The other guard agreed. "But be careful. Easterners are fragile. Remember the last one."

"I'll be careful." He looked at me and smiled. "Last chance," he said. "What do you know about those two dead men outside?"

I shook my head, which hurt like blazes, but I knew trying to talk would hurt more. He hefted his dagger, hilt up, and swung his arm back for a good windup. . . .

I don't know how long the whole thing lasted. It was certainly one of the worst I'd been through, but if they'd chosen to take me back to their barracks it would have been worse. Phoenix Guards are never *ordered* to beat up Jhereg, or Easterners, or anyone else, but some of them don't like us.

This beating was peculiar. I'd been bashed around before; it was one of the prices I paid for living according to my own rules instead of the Empire's. But why this time? The two dead men were Jhereg, and the usual attitude of Imperial Guards to such things is: let 'em kill each other off, for all we care. It could have been just another excuse to beat up an Easterner or a Jhereg, but they'd seemed genuinely angry about something.

These thoughts came to me through a thick haze of pain as I was lying on my office floor. I was concentrating as hard as I could on figuring out the reason behind the beating so that I could avoid thinking about how every inch of me hurt. I could tell there were people around me, but I couldn't open my eyes to see who they were, and they were talking in whispers.

After a time, I heard Melestav say, "Here she is, move back," followed by the sound of a long garment dragging across the floor. This was followed by a gasp. I decided I must be quite a sight.

The newcomer said, "Get away from him." I recognized, with surprise and some relief, Aliera's voice. I tried to force my eyes to open, but they wouldn't.

I heard Kragar say, "How bad is he, Aliera?" but she chose not to answer him. That didn't necessarily mean that I was in bad shape; Aliera so utterly despised Kragar that she preferred not to speak to him whenever possible.

"Kragar . . ."

"Are you all right, Vlad?"

"No, but never mind that. They seemed mad about something in particular. Any idea what?"

"Yeah. While they were . . . while they were here, I got Daymar to do a mind-probe."

"Kragar, you know I don't like Daymar to know—never mind. What did he find out?"

We were interrupted by Aliera saying, "Sleep, Vlad." I was going to argue, but I discovered that she wasn't just making a suggestion. I saw a pale green light, and I slept.

Aliera was there when I woke up again, as was the picture of the dzur and the jhereg. This led to the realization that I could see again. I took stock of my various body parts, and found that, while I still hurt, it was mostly dull aches instead of flaming agony. Aliera is a very good healer.

"I might as well move in here," I said.

"I heard what happened, Vlad," said Aliera. "On behalf of the House of the Dragon, I apologize."

I grunted.

"The one who beat you—his name is Menthar? He is off duty in four months."

I felt my eyes trying to widen. I studied her. Her lips were pressed tightly together, and her eyes were gray. Her hands were in fists, at her sides. "Four months," she repeated, "and then he's fair game."

"Thank you," I said. "I appreciate the information."

She nodded. Dragonlords were Dragonlords, and usually hated Jhereg and Easterners both—but they didn't approve of attacking people who couldn't defend themselves, and Aliera knew enough about how the Jhereg operated to know that if a representative of the Empire wanted to knock around a Jhereg, the Jhereg would just have to take it. But, I suppose, there's something about being in the guard, and watching us get away with everything we get away with, that frustrates them. For my part, I didn't feel any moral outrage at what had happened to me. I just wanted to tear that guy's arms off. . . . Four months.

"Thank you," I said again. "I think I want to sleep now."

"Good," she said. "I'll be back in a while."

She left and I got in touch with Kragar. *"You were saying?"*

"Vlad! How are you?"

"About how you'd expect. Now, what did Daymar find out?"

"The guards were pulled out the other day because they were needed somewhere else. There was a riot in the Easterners' Quarter. That may explain why those two took it out on you. I suppose they aren't happy with any Easterners now. There have been other beatings of Easterners in the last few days. A few have been beaten to death."

"I see. It can't have been very big or we'd have heard about it."

"No. It was small, short, and pretty bloody, from what Daymar could tell. I'm checking into it, just on general principles."

"Okay, so that mystery is solved. Now: who set off the riot? Laris, I suppose. We need to find out how he has influence around there. That's quite a bit farther south than anything else he has."

"Okay. I'll see if we can find out. Don't expect much, though."

"I won't. Anything yet on that other business?"

"A bit, but not enough to help, I don't think. Her name is Norathar, and she's of the e'Lanya line. I've found references to her being expelled from the House, but no details—yet."

"Good. Keep working on it. Next point: how can Laris afford to keep assassins sitting outside the office?"

"Well, didn't you say the Sword and the Dagger had returned their payment?"

"Yeah. But that begs the question. How could he afford to hire them? Plus pay whatever it must have cost to start trouble in the Easterners' Quarter?"

"Uh... I don't know. I guess he has more cash than we thought."

"Right. But how did he get it?"

"Maybe the same way you did?"

"That's just what I was thinking. Maybe he's being supported by someone who's rich."

"It could be, Vlad."

"So, let's look into it."

"Sure. How do we do that?"

"I don't know. Think about it."

"Check. And, Vlad..."

"Yeah?"

"Next time you come back here, warn us first, okay?"

"Yeah."

After breaking that contact, I got hold of Fentor at Castle Black, gave him the information about the riot, and asked him to find out what he could about it. Then I really did sleep.

"Wake up, boss!"

It was like the drumbeat that sends a squadron into alert status. I was sitting up, holding a dagger under the blanket, looking at—

"Good afternoon, Vladimir. Is that a knife in your hand, or are you happy to see me?"

"Both," I said, sheathing the blade. She tapped my side and I moved over to let her sit down. We exchanged a light kiss. She drew back and studied me.

"What happened?"

"It's a long story."

"I've got nothing but time."

I told her what had happened. She shook her head and, when I was finished, held me.

Wow.

"What now?" she asked.

I said, "Do you and your partner ever give friends a bargain?"

"Do you?"

"I didn't think so."

She held me a little tighter.

"Would you two rather I left, boss?"

"Maybe in a bit."

"Hmmph. I was being snide, if you didn't notice."

"I noticed. Shut up."

"By the way, Vladimir, Sethra is giving a banquet."

"Really? In honor of what?"

"In honor of all of us being alive."

"Hmmmm. They'll probably be trying to pump you and Norathar for information."

"I expect they—how did you find out her name?"

I did a smug chuckle.

"I guess," she said, "I'll just have to torture the information out of you."

"I guess so," I said. *"Okay, Loiosh, you can leave now."*

"Jerk."

"Yeah."

10.

"I dislike killing my guests."

It is possible to break meals down into types. There is the formal dinner, with elegant settings, carefully selected wines, and orchestrated conversation. Then there are Jhereg business meetings, where you ignore the food half the time, because to miss a remark, or even a glance, can be deadly. There is the quiet, informal get-together with a Certain Person, where neither food nor conversation is as important as being there. We also have the grab-something-and-run, where the idea is to get food inside of you, without taking time for either conversation or enjoyment. Next, we have the "good dinner," where the food is the whole reason for being there, and conversation is merely to help wash it down.

And there is one other type of dinner: sitting around a fine, elegant table, deep under Dzur Mountain, with an undead hostess, a pair of Dragonlords, and a team of Jhereg assassins, one of whom was once a Dragon herself, the other of whom is an Easterner.

The conversation at a dinner of this type is unpredictable.

For most of the meal, Morrolan entertained us with a few notes on sorcery that aren't usually included in tomes, and probably shouldn't be. I enjoyed this—mostly because I was sitting next to Cawti (by chance? With Aliera around? Ha!) and we generally concentrated on rubbing our legs together under the table. Loiosh made a few remarks about this that I won't dignify by repeating.

Then, while I was distracted, the conversation changed. Suddenly, Aliera was engaging the lady known as the Sword of the Jhereg in a bantering exchange comparing Dragon customs to Jhereg customs, and I was instantly alert. Aliera didn't do *anything* by accident.

"You see," Aliera was saying, "we only kill people who deserve it. You kill anyone you're paid to kill."

Norathar pretended surprise. "But you're paid too, aren't you? It's merely a different coin. A Jhereg assassin would be paid in gold, or so I assume—I've never actually met one. A Dragon, on the other hand, is paid by satisfying his bloodlust."

I chuckled a little. Score one for our team. Aliera also smiled and raised her glass. I looked at her closely. Yes, I decided, she wasn't doing any idle Jhereg-baiting. She was searching for something.

"So tell me," Aliera asked, "which do you consider the better coin to be paid in?"

"Well, I've never bought anything with bloodlust, but—"

"It can be done."

"Indeed? What can you buy, pray tell?"

"Empires," said Aliera e'Kieron. "Empires."

Norathar e'Lanya raised her eyebrow. "Empires, my lady? What would I do with one?"

Aliera shrugged. "I'm sure you could think of something."

I glanced around the room. Sethra, at the head of the table and to my right, was watching Aliera intently. Morrolan, to her right, was doing the same. Norathar was next to him, and she was also studying Aliera, who was at the other end of the table. Cawti, next to her and to my left, was looking at Norathar. I wondered what was going on behind her mask. I always wonder what's going on behind people's masks. I sometimes wonder what's going on behind *my* mask.

"What would you do with one?" asked Norathar.

"Ask me when the Cycle changes."

"Eh?"

"I," she said, "am currently the Dragon Heir to the Throne. Morrolan used to be, before I arrived."

I remembered being told about Aliera's "arrival"—hurled out of Adron's Disaster, the explosion that brought down the Empire over four hundred years ago, through time, to land in the middle of some Teckla's wheat field. I was later told that Sethra had had a hand in the thing, which made it more believable than it would be otherwise.

Norathar seemed faintly curious. Her eyes went to the Dragonhead pendant around Aliera's neck. All Dragonlords wear a Dragonhead somewhere visible. The one Aliera wore had a blue gem for one eye, a green gem for the other. "E'Kieron, I see," said Norathar.

Aliera nodded, as if something had been explained.

I asked, "What am I missing?"

"The lady," said Aliera, "was no doubt curious about my lineage, and why I am now the heir. I would guess that she has remembered that Adron had a daughter."

I said, "Oh."

It had never occurred to me to wonder how Aliera came to be the heir so quickly, although I'd known she was since I was introduced to her. But sitting at the same table with the daughter of the man who had turned an entire city into a seething pool of raw chaos was a bit disconcerting. I decided it was going to take me a while to get used to.

Aliera continued her explanations to Norathar. "The Dragon Council informed me of the decision when they checked my bloodlines. That is how I became interested in genetics. I am hoping that I can prove there is a flaw in me, somewhere, so I won't have to be Empress when the Cycle changes."

"You mean you don't *want* to be Empress?" I asked.

"Dear Barlen, no! I can't imagine anything more dull. I've been looking for a way out of it since I've been back."

"Oh."

"Your conversation is really gifted today, boss."

"Shut up, Loiosh."

I worked all of this over in my mind. "Aliera," I said at last, "I have a question."

"Hm?"

"If you're the Dragon Heir, does that mean your father was the heir before you? And if he *was* the heir, why did he try the coup in the first place?"

"Two reasons," she said. "First, because it was the reign of a decadent Phoenix, and the Emperor refused to step down when the Cycle changed. Second, Daddy wasn't really the heir."

"Oh. The heir died during the Interregnum?"

"Around then, yes. There was a war, and he was killed. There was talk of his child not being a Dragon. But that was actually before the Disaster and the Interregnum.

"He was killed," I echoed. "I see. And the child? No, don't tell me. She was expelled from the House, right?"

Aliera nodded.

"And the line? E'Lanya, right?"

"Very good, Vlad. How did you know?"

I looked at Norathar, who was staring at Aliera with eyes like mushrooms.

"And," I continued, "you have been able to scan her genes, and you've found out that, lo and behold, she really *is* a Dragonlord."

"Yes," said Aliera.

"And if her father was really the Heir to the Throne, then..."

"That's right, Vlad," said Aliera. "The correct Heir to the Throne is Norathar e'Lanya—the Sword of the Jhereg."

The funniest thing about time is when it doesn't. I'll leave that hanging there for the moment, and let you age while the shadows don't lengthen, if you see what I mean.

I looked first at Cawti, who was looking at Norathar,

who was looking at Aliera. Sethra and Morrolan were also looking at Aliera, who wasn't focusing on anything we could see. Her eyes, bright green now, glittered with reflected candlelight, and looked upon something we weren't entitled to see.

Now, while the Cycle doesn't turn, and the year doesn't fail, and the day gets neither brighter nor darker, and even the candles don't flicker, we begin to see things with a new perspective. I looked first at my lover, who had recently killed me, who was looking at her partner, who should be the Dragon Heir to the Orb—next in the Cycle. This Dragonlord-assassin-princess-whatever matched stares with Aliera e'Kieron, wielder of Kieron's Sword, traveler from the past, daughter of Adron, and current Heir to the Orb. And so on.

The funniest thing about time is when it doesn't. In those moments when it loses itself, and becomes (as, perhaps, all things must) its opposite, it becomes a thing of even greater power than when it is in its old standard tear-down-the-mountains mood.

It even has the power to break down the masks behind which hide Dragons turned Jhereg.

For an instant, then, I looked at Norathar and saw her clearly, she who had once been a Dragonlord. I saw pride, hate, grim resignation, dashed hopes, loyalty, and courage. I turned away, though, because, odd as it may seem to you who have listened to me so patiently and so well, I really don't like pain.

"What do you mean?" she whispered, and the world went back to its business again.

Aliera didn't answer, so Sethra spoke. "The Dragon Council met, early in the Reign of the Phoenix this Cycle, before the Interregnum, to choose the heir. It was decided that the e'Lanya line should take it when the time comes. The highest family of that line were the Lady Miera, the Lord K'laiyer, and their daughter, Norathar."

Norathar shook her head and whispered again. "I have no memories of any of this. I was only a child."

"There was an accusation made," said Sethra, "and Lord

K'laiyer, your father, challenged his accuser. There was war, and your parents were killed. You were judged by sorcerers and your bloodlines were found to be impure."

"But then—"

"Aliera scanned you, and the sorcerers who made the first judgment were wrong."

I broke in, saying, "How hard is it to make a mistake of that kind?"

Aliera snapped back to the present and said, "Impossible."

"I see," I said.

"I see," said Norathar.

We sat there, each of us looking down, or around the room, waiting for someone to ask the obvious questions. Finally, Norathar did. "Who did the scan, and who made the challenge?"

"The first scan," said Sethra, "was done by my apprentice, Sethra the Younger."

"Who's she?" I asked.

"As I said, my apprentice—one of many. She served her apprenticeship—let me see—about twelve hundred years ago now. When I'd taught her all I could, she did me the honor of taking my name."

"Dragonlord?"

"Of course."

"Okay. Sorry to interrupt. You were talking about the scan."

"Yes. She brought the results to me, and I brought them to the Dragon Council. The council had a committee of three do another one. Lord Baritt was one—" Morrolan, Aliera and I exchanged glances here. We'd met his shade in the Paths of the Dead, and had three completely different impressions of the old bas- . . . gentleman. Sethra continued. "Another was of the House of the Athyra, as the expert, and someone from the House of the Lyorn, to make sure everything was right and proper. The committee confirmed it and the council acted as it had to."

Norathar asked, "Who made the accusation?"

"I did," said Sethra Lavode.

• • •

Norathar rose to her feet, her eyes burning into Sethra's. I could almost feel the energy flowing between them. Norathar said, between clenched teeth, "May I have my sword back, milady?"

Sethra hadn't moved. "If you wish," she said. "However, there are two things I want to say."

"Say them."

"First, I made the accusation because that was my duty to the House of the Dragon as I saw it. Second, while I'm not as fanatical about it as Lord Morrolan, I dislike killing my guests. Remember who I am, lady!"

As she said this, she stood and drew Iceflame—a long, straight dagger, perhaps twelve inches of blade. The metal was a light blue, and it emitted a faint glow of that color. Anyone with the psionic sensitivity of a caterpillar would have recognized it as a Morganti weapon, one which kills without chance of revivification. Anyone with any acquaintance with the legends surrounding Sethra Lavode would have recognized it as Iceflame, a Great Weapon, one of the Seventeen. Whatever power it was that hid in, under, and around Dzur Mountain, Iceflame was tied to it. The only other known artifacts with power to match it were the sword Godslayer and the Imperial Orb. Loiosh dived under my cloak. I held my breath.

At that moment, I felt, rather than saw, a knife fall into Cawti's hand. I felt a tear in loyalties that was almost physically painful. What should I do if there was a fight? Could I bring myself to stop Cawti, or even warn Sethra? Could I bring myself to allow Sethra to be knifed in the back? Demon Goddess, get me out of this!

Norathar stared back at Sethra and said, "Cawti, don't." Cawti sighed quietly, and I breathed a prayer of thanks to Verra. Then Norathar said to Sethra, "I'd like my sword, if you please."

"You won't hear my reasons, then?" asked Sethra, her voice even.

"All right," said Norathar. "Speak."

"Thank you." Sethra put Iceflame away. I exhaled. Sethra

sat down and, after a moment, so did Norathar, but her eyes never left Sethra's.

"I was told," said the Dark Lady of Dzur Mountain, "that your ancestry was questionable. To be blunt, I received word that you were a bastard. I'm sorry, but that's what I was told."

I listened intently. Bastardy among Dragaerans is far more rare than among Easterners, because a Dragaeran can't conceive accidentally—or so I've been told. In general, the only illegitimate children are those who have one sterile parent (sterility is nearly impossible to cure, and not uncommon among Dragaerans). *Bastard,* as an insult, is far more deadly to a Dragaeran than to an Easterner.

"I was further told," she continued, "that your true father was not a Dragon." Norathar still didn't move, but she was gripping the table with her right hand. "You were the oldest child of the Dragon Heir. It was necessary to bring this to the attention of the council, if it was true.

"I could," she went on, "have sneaked into your parents' home with my apprentice, who is skilled in genetic scanning." Aliera gave a barely audible sniff here. I imagine she had her own opinion of Sethra the Younger's abilities. "I chose not to, however. I confronted Lord K'laiyer. He held himself insulted and refused to allow the scan. He declared war and sent an army after me."

She sighed. "I've lost count of how many armies have tried to take Dzur Mountain. If it's any consolation, he was a masterful tactician, certainly worthy of the e'Lanya line. But I had the assistance of several friends, a hired army, and Dzur Mountain itself. He gave me a bit of trouble, but the issue was never in doubt. By the end of the engagement, both of your parents were dead."

"How?" asked Norathar through clenched teeth. A good question, too. Why weren't they revivified?

"I don't know. They were in the battle, but I didn't kill them personally. They both had massive head injuries, due to sorcery. Beyond that, I can't tell you."

Norathar nodded, almost imperceptibly. Sethra continued. "I formally took possession of their castle, of course.

We found you there. You were about four years old, I think. I had my apprentice do the scan, and you know the rest. I turned your castle over to the House. I don't know what became of it, or your parents' possessions. Perhaps there are relatives. . . ."

Norathar nodded again. "Thank you," she said. "But this hardly changes—"

"There's another thing. If my apprentice made a mistake, it reflects on me. Further, it is obvious that my actions were the immediate cause of all this. I trust Aliera's abilities with genetics more than anyone else's—and she says you are the product of Dragonlords on both sides, with e'Lanya dominant. I want to know what happened. I intend to investigate. If I kill you, that will make it more difficult. If you destroy me, of course, that will make it impossible. I would appreciate it if you would withhold any challenge until I've made this investigation. Then, if you wish, I will entertain a challenge on any terms you name."

"Any terms?" asked Norathar. "Including plain steel?"

Sethra snorted. "Including a Jhereg duel, if you wish."

The least shadow of a smile crossed Norathar's lips as she seated herself. "I accept your terms," she said. Cawti and I relaxed. Morrolan and Aliera, as far as I could tell, had been interested but unworried.

Morrolan cleared his throat and said, "Well then, perhaps we should discuss just how we're going to proceed."

Sethra said, "Tell me this: if there was a plot of some kind, could Baritt have been involved?"

Aliera said "No" at the same instant that Morrolan said "Yes." I chuckled. Aliera shrugged and said, "Well, maybe."

Morrolan snorted. "In any case," he said, "is it likely that they could fool an Athyra? And would an Athyra be involved in a plot of this type? Not to mention a Lyorn? If this was a plot, as you say, they would have had to convince the Athyra to help, and I have trouble believing they could do that. And there is no Lyorn in the world who would go along with it—that is why they're included in things like that."

Sethra nodded to herself.

I said, "Excuse me, but what is the procedure for getting a Lyorn and an Athyra to help with something like this? I mean, do you just walk over to the House of the Lyorn and yell, 'We're doing a genetic investigation, anyone want to help?' What do you do?"

Sethra said, "With the House of the Lyorn, it is an official request, through the Empire, for the assistance of the House. With the Athyra, someone will propose a wizard he knows or has heard of, and the council approves it."

"And the House of the Lyorn is likely to choose someone who's familiar with this kind of thing," I added.

Sethra nodded.

"Okay," I said. "But—Aliera, how hard would it be to fool a genetic scan?"

"A complicated illusion spell would do it," she said slowly. "*If* whoever did the scan was incompetent."

"What if he wasn't?"

"He wouldn't be fooled."

"Could Sethra the Younger be fooled?"

"Easily." She snorted.

I shot a glance at Sethra Lavode; she didn't seem convinced. I set it aside for the moment. "What about Baritt?"

"No," said Aliera.

Morrolan agreed. "Whatever he is—was—he was most assuredly *not* incompetent."

"So," I continued, "if someone did a spell to make it look like she wasn't a full Dragon, Baritt must have been in on it. The Lyorn could have been fooled."

"Vlad," said Morrolan, "the Athyra would have to have been in on it, too—and you'll have to convince me of that."

"I haven't figured that out yet," I admitted. "But one thing at a time. Sethra, how did Sethra the Younger first hear about this?"

"I don't know, Vlad. It was more than four hundred years ago."

"At your age, Sethra, that's almost yesterday."

She raised an eyebrow. Then her eyes moved up and to the left as she tried to remember. "She said that she heard through a friend who'd been drinking with Lady Miera. She said that Lady Miera had told her friend about it, and her friend told her."

"And the friend's name?"

She sighed and leaned back in her chair. She rested her hands on top of her head, leaned her head back, and rolled her eyes straight up. We sat there, hardly daring to breathe. Suddenly she straightened up. "Vlad, it was Baritt!"

Why, I wondered, doesn't this surprise me?

I shook my head. "If you people want to find out what Baritt knows about this, I can tell you where to find him, but don't expect me to go along with you. I've been to Deathsgate once; that will last a lifetime—at least. I've got my own problems. There's a guy who's trying to send me there. Figuratively speaking," I added. "I understand they don't allow Easterners in.

"Anyway," I continued, "Sethra, do you remember who the Lyorn was?"

"I never knew," she said. "My part of it was over, and I wanted nothing more to do with it. I wasn't along when they did the second scan."

"Oh. So I suppose you don't know who the Athyra was, either."

"Right."

"It'll all be in the records," Aliera put in. "We can find out."

I nodded. "Then I don't think there's anything more to do about this at the moment, right?"

There were nods from Sethra, Aliera, and Morrolan. Norathar and Cawti had been watching us the entire time without any expression. It occurred to me that it was odd for me to have taken the lead in this investigation into the history of the House of the Dragon. But then, in a certain sense, investigation is one of the things I'm good at. Cawti could have done it as well, but she had even less interest than I did.

"The next question," said Morrolan, "is how we're going to present this to the Dragon Council. I would suggest that Aliera and I appear before them and—"

Aliera interrupted. "Perhaps later would be better for this.

It's really a matter to be discussed among Dragons."

There was a brief, uncomfortable silence; then Cawti stood up. "Excuse me," she said. "I believe that I'd like to retire now."

Sethra stood and bowed an acknowledgment as Cawti left. Then Sethra sat down again, and Morrolan said, "I wonder what troubles her?"

Typical.

"The end of a partnership," Norathar said, and it seemed that there were new lines of pain around her eyes and jaw. But then, she was a Dragonlord now, so she could show her feelings. She stood, bowed, and followed Cawti out of the room.

I followed them with my eyes, then glanced at the table. The food was cold and the wine was warm. If there had been an onion, it would have been rotten clear through.

11.

"A quick game, boss?"

They left me alone at the table, so I thought about onions for a while. I was still thinking about them when I felt someone reaching for me psionically.

"Who is it?"

"Fentor, at Castle Black, milord. I have the information you wanted."

"On the riot? Good, let's have it."

"It was confined to three blocks, near—"

"I know where it was. Go on."

"Yes, milord. It was a row of flats, all owned by the same person. He'd started raising rents about four weeks before, and letting things deteriorate, and then began beating Easterners who were slow in paying."

"I see. Who owned the flats?"

"A Jhereg, lord. His name is—"

"Laris."

"Yes, milord."

I sighed. *"Had he owned the property for long?"*

There was a pause. *"It didn't occur to me to check, lord."*

"Do so. And find out who he bought it from."

"Yes, milord."

"Is there anything more?"

"Not yet, milord, but we're still working on it."

"Good. Another thing, too: I suspect someone triggered the riot deliberately. Try to find out."

"Yes, milord."

We broke the contact. The conversation made me realize, among other things, that I'd been neglecting my own affairs again. I got in touch with Kragar and told him to expect me in two minutes. Then I made contact with Sethra, explained that I had to leave, and would she be good enough to teleport me back to my office? She would and did.

I didn't have to tell her where it was, either. Sometimes I wonder about her.

Kragar was waiting for me, along with Glowbug and someone I didn't recognize. We went into the still-unrepaired building, and I told Kragar to come into the office with me. I shut the door, looked around, and didn't see him. I opened up the door again and said, "Kragar, I said to—"

"Boss?"

I turned, and saw him this time.

"Damn it, Kragar, stop *doing* that."

"Doing what, Vlad?"

"Never mind. *Cut it out, Loiosh."*

"I didn't say a thing, boss."

"You were laughing up your wing."

I sat down and put my feet up on the desk. "Who's the new guy?"

"An enforcer. We need another one, and we can almost afford it. He knows he's staying on subject to your approval."

"What's his name?"

"Stadol."

"Never heard of him."

"He's called 'Sticks.'"

"Oh. So *that's* Sticks." I yelled, "Melestav, send Sticks in."

The door opened and he walked in.

"Sit," I told him.

He did.

Sticks might have gotten his name because he looked like one, but that can be said of almost all Dragaerans. Still, he was taller and thinner than most, and carried himself as if every bone in his body were jelly. His arms swung easily when he walked, and his knees sagged a bit. He had sandy hair, straight, and worn to his ears. One lock dangled over his forehead and looked like it would get in his eyes. He periodically threw his head to the side to clear it, but it flopped down almost right away.

In fact, the nickname came from his preference for using two three-foot clubs. He beat people up with them.

I said, "I'm Vlad Taltos." He nodded. "You want to work for me?"

"Sure," he said. "The money's good."

"That's because things are hot right now. You know about that?"

He nodded again.

"You ever 'work'?"

"No. No future in it."

"That's debatable. I've heard of you doing some muscle a few years back. What have you been doing since?"

He shrugged. "I have some connections with a few minstrels, and with some taverns. I help introduce them, and they give me a percentage. It's a living."

"Then why leave it?"

"No future in it."

". . . Okay. You're in."

"Thanks."

"That's it for now."

He made a slow climb to his feet and ambled out. I turned back to Kragar. It took me a moment to find him, then I asked him: "Anything new?"

"No. I'm working on the patron angle, but I haven't come up with anything."

"Keep on it."

"Right."

"Get Narvane and Shoen here."

"Right."

He got hold of them and we sat back to wait. While we were waiting . . .

"Milord?"

"Yes, Fentor?"

"You were right. There was someone who provoked the riot. It looks deliberate."

"Pick him up and hold him. I'm going to want to—"

"We can't, milord."

"Dead?"

"Yes, milord. In the riot."

'I see. Chance, or was someone after him?"

"I can't tell, milord."

"All right. What about the previous landlord?"

"The Jhereg Laris has owned those flats for about nine weeks, milord. We don't know who he bought them from. The records are confused, and there seems to have been some false names used."

"Untangle it."

"Yes, milord."

"What was that?" asked Kragar when I broke the contact.

I shook my head and didn't answer. He stood, went to my closet, and came back with a box. "You asked for these."

The box contained a rather large selection of cutlery, of various sorts. Seeing them gathered together like that, I was a little amazed that I could fit it all around my person. I mean, there were—no, I don't think I want to give the specifics.

I thought about sending Kragar out while I changed weapons, then decided against it. I picked up the first thing I came to, a small throwing knife, tested its edge and balance, and put it into my cloak in place of the one like it that I had there.

It was surprising how long it took to go through all the weapons I carried and replace them. When I'd finally finished the chore, Narvane and Shoen were waiting. As I stepped out of the office, I ran a hand through my hair and adjusted my cloak with the other hand, thus allowing me to brush my arms along my chest, making sure various things were in place. A very useful nervous gesture.

Narvane acknowledged me with a flicker of the eyes. Shoen nodded brusquely. Sticks, flopped all over a chair, lifted a hand, and Glowbug said, "Good to see you, boss. I was beginning to think you were a myth."

"If you're beginning to think, Glowbug, it's an improvement already. Let's go, gentlemen."

This time, Loiosh was the first one out of the door, followed by Glowbug and Narvane. The other two followed me, leaving Kragar behind. We turned left and headed up to Malak Circle. I said hello to a few customers I knew personally, and to some people who worked for me. I got the impression that, in the last day, business had picked up. This was a considerable relief. There was still a feeling of tension in the air, but it was more in the background.

We reached the Fountain Tavern, then the first door to the left. "Sticks," I said.

"Hm?"

"This is where the trouble started. Laris opened up a small business upstairs, without even dropping me a polite note about it."

"Mm."

"For all I know, it's still going on. Glowbug and Shoen will wait out here with me."

"Okay."

He turned and went up the stairs. Narvane followed wordlessly. As they went in, I saw Sticks pulling a pair of clubs out from his cloak. I leaned against the building to wait. Glowbug and Shoen stood in front of me, to either side, casually alert.

"Watch above, Loiosh."

"I'm already doing it, boss."

It wasn't long before we heard a crash from up and to the right. We looked, and a body came flying out the window, landing in a heap about ten feet from me. A minute or so later, Narvane and Sticks reappeared. Sticks was holding something in his left fist. With the club in the other hand, he drew a series of squares in the dirt in front of me.

I looked at him questioningly, but before he could say anything, I noticed a crowd had begun to gather around the body. I gave them all a smile.

Sticks opened his left hand then, and dropped several stones, some white, some black, onto the squares he'd drawn in the street.

"A quick game, boss?"

"No thanks," I told him. "I don't gamble."

He nodded sagaciously. "No future in it," he said. We continued on around the circle.

Eventually, I returned to my office; I was pleased to be able to tell Kragar to expect an increase in our take this week. He grunted.

"Do something for me, Kragar."

"What?"

"Go visit that guy who told us about the setup. Find out if he knows anything more."

"Visit him? Personally?"

"Yeah. Face to face and all that."

"Why?"

"I don't know. Maybe to find out if he's unusual, so we can guess if we're going to get any other takers."

He shrugged. "All right. But won't that be putting him in danger?"

"Not if no one notices you."

He grunted again. "All right. When?"

"Now will be fine."

He sighed, which was a welcome relief from the grunts, and left.

"Now what, Loiosh?"

"Got me, boss. Find Laris?"

"I'd love to. How? If he weren't protected against witchcraft, I'd just try to nail him where he is."

"It works out even, boss. If we weren't protected against sorcery, he'd *nail* us *where we are."*

"I suppose. Hey, Loiosh."

"Yeah, boss?"

"I feel like I've been, I don't know, brushing you off

lately, when I've been around Cawti. I'm sorry."

His tongue flicked against the inside of my ear. *"It's okay, boss. I understand. Besides, one of these days, I'll probably find someone myself."*

"I hope so. I think. Tell me something: have I been off *recently? I mean, this business with Cawti, do you think it's been getting in my way? I feel like I've been distracted or something."*

"A little, maybe. Don't worry about it. You've been doing all right when things get rough, and I don't think there's anything you can do about it anyway."

"Yeah. You know, Loiosh, I'm glad you're around."

"Aw, shucks, boss."

Kragar returned about two hours later.

"Well?"

"I'm not sure if I learned anything useful or not, Vlad. He doesn't have any idea where Laris is, but he's willing to tell us if he finds out. He was pretty nervous about meeting me, but that's understandable. Well, not *nervous,* exactly. Surprised, maybe, and caught off guard. Anyway, he hadn't heard anything that struck me as useful."

"Hmmmm. Did you get any feel for whether there might be others like him?"

Kragar shook his head.

"Okay," I admitted, "I guess that didn't get us anywhere. How about our other sources? Have we found anyone else who works for Laris?"

"A couple. But we can't do anything about them until we have more funds. Paying for 'work' would break us right now."

"Just two days until Endweek. Maybe we'll be able to do something then. Leave me alone for a while now. I want to think."

He made an exit. I leaned back, closed my eyes, and was interrupted again.

"Milord?"

"What is it, Fentor?"

"We found out part of it. The flats had belonged to a Dragonlord who died, and they've been sort of kicking around since then."

"How long ago did he die?"

"About two years ago, milord."

"I see. And you can't find out who got possession after that?"

"Not yet, milord."

"Keep working on it. Who was the Dragon, by the way?"

"A powerful sorcerer, lord. He was called Baritt."

Well now.... By all the Lords of Judgment, how was I going to fit *this* into my thinking? Coincidence came to mind, was thrown away, and kept coming back. How could it be coincidence? How could it *not* be coincidence?

"Milord?"

"Fentor, find out everything you can about that, right away. Put more people on it. Break into Imperial records, bribe recordsmiths, whatever you have to, but find out."

"Yes, milord."

Baritt... Baritt....

A powerful sorcerer, a wizard, a Dragonlord. He was old when he died, and had made such a name for himself that he was no longer referred to by his lineage. Rather, his descendants referred to themselves as "e'Baritt." He had died only two years ago, and his monument, near Deathsgate Falls, had been the site of the bloodiest battle since the Interregnum.

Baritt.

It was easy enough to imagine him involved in some sort of conspiracy within the House of the Dragon, but what could he have to do with the Jhereg? Could *he* be Laris's patron? Or could one of his descendants be? If so, why?

What's more, if there was a relationship between my problem with Laris and Norathar's problem with Baritt, that meant a deep intrigue of some kind, and Dragonlords simply *aren't* intriguers—with the possible exception of Aliera, and then only within a limited sphere.

Was I really going to have to visit Deathsgate Falls and the Paths of the Dead again? I shuddered. Remembering my last visit, I knew that those who dwell there would not take my coming again at all kindly. Would it do any good if I did? Probably not; Baritt had certainly not been well disposed toward me last time.

But it *couldn't* be coincidence. His name turning up like that, owning the very flats that had been used by Laris. Why hadn't they merely passed to his heirs? Because someone had played with the records? Maybe, which would explain why Fentor was having so much trouble tracking down the ownership. But then, who? Why?

I reached out for contact with Morrolan.

"Yes, Vlad?"

"Tell me about Baritt."

"Hmmph."

"I already knew that."

"Precisely what do you wish to know, Vlad?"

"How did he die?"

"Eh? You don't know?"

"If I knew—no, I don't know."

"He was assassinated."

Oh. That at least explained some of the remarks he'd made to me.

"I see. How was it done? I'm surprised a sorcerer as skilled as Baritt would allow himself to be cut down."

"Hmmm. As I recall, Vlad, there is a saying among you Jhereg . . ."

"Ah. Yes. 'No matter how subtle the wizard, a knife between the shoulder blades will seriously cramp his style.' "

"Yes."

"So it was a Jhereg?"

"What other assassins do you know of?"

"There are plenty of amateurs who'll knife anyone for five gold. A Jhereg will hardly ever 'work' on anyone who isn't in the House; there usually isn't any need to, unless someone is threatening to go to the Empire about something, or—"

I stopped dead.

Morrolan said, *"Yes, Vlad? Or . . . ?"*

I let him hang there. Or, I had been about to say, unless

it's done as a special favor, set up by a Jhereg, for a friend from another House. Which meant that maybe, *maybe* it hadn't been Baritt behind the whole thing, after all. Maybe he'd been working with whoever it was, and this other person then needed Baritt taken out. And this other person was Laris's patron. And, since Laris had helped out with Baritt, his patron was ready to help Laris get rid of me. A simple exchange of favors.

"Vlad?"

"Sorry, Morrolan, I'm trying to figure something out. Bide a moment, please."

"Very well."

So Laris's patron was someone who had been working with Baritt about two years ago. Yes. Who would know?

"Morrolan, who would be likely to know someone who was working with Baritt shortly before his death?"

"I'm not sure, Vlad. I don't know, myself. We never had much to do with each other while he was alive. Perhaps you should show up at Castle Black and ask around."

"Yes . . . perhaps I'll do that. Well, thank you. I'll talk to you later."

"Certainly, Vlad."

Well, well, and well.

At the very least, Laris was in it with someone else, and this someone else, presumably a Dragonlord, was helping him against me. If I could find out who he was, I might be able to nullify him simply by threatening to expose him; Dragons don't think highly of their own kind helping out Jhereg.

Finding him involved discovering who had owned those flats. Hmmm. I reached out for—

"Fentor."

"Yes, milord?"

"Make a list of every currently living descendant of Baritt. Have it ready in an hour."

"An hour, milord?"

"Yes."

"But—yes, milord."

I broke the link, and opened another one.

"Who is it?"

"Hello, Sethra."

"Oh, Vlad. Good evening. What can I do for you?"

"Is it still necessary to hold Norathar and Cawti prisoner?"

"I was just discussing that with Aliera. Why?"

"It would be helpful if Cawti were free this evening."

"I see." There was a pause, then: *"Very well, Vlad. Neither Aliera nor Morrolan objects."*

"You'll release both of them?"

"The Easterner was the only one in doubt. Norathar, as far as we're concerned, is a Dragon."

"I see. Well, thank you."

"You're welcome. I'll tell them at once."

"Make it five minutes from now, all right?"

"If you wish."

"Thank you."

Then I took a deep breath and began concentrating on Cawti, whom I didn't really know all that well. But I thought about her face, her voice, her—

"Vladimir!"

"Got it on the first guess. What are you doing tonight?"

"What am I—? What do you suppose I'm doing? Your friends still haven't allowed us to leave."

"I think that can be arranged. If so, would the lady be so kind as to allow me to escort her to a small gathering this evening?"

"I should be honored, most gracious lord."

"Excellent. Then I'll see you in an hour."

"I'll be looking forward to it."

I broke the contact and yelled for my bodyguards to escort me home, so I could get properly dressed for the occasion. It doesn't do to underdress for Castle Black.

12

"Friendly, isn't she?"

Two teleports after leaving home I was at Castle Black with Cawti and an unsteady stomach. Cawti was dressed to kill in long trousers of light gray, a blouse of the same color, and a gray cloak with black trim. I wore my good trousers, my good jerkin, and my cloak. We looked like a matched set.

Lady Teldra admitted us, greeted Cawti by name, and bade us visit the banquet hall. We must have been quite a sight: a pair of Easterners, both in Jhereg colors, with Loiosh on my left shoulder, putting him between us.

No one particularly noticed us.

I reached Fentor and told him where I was. He showed up, found me, and surreptitiously handed me a slip of paper. After he left, Cawti and I wandered around for a bit, seeing people and studying Morrolan's "dining room," and being casually insulted by passersby. After a while, I introduced her to the Necromancer.

Cawti bowed from the neck, which is subtly different than bowing the head. The Necromancer seemed uninterested, but returned the bow. The Necromancer didn't care whether you were a Dragaeran or an Easterner, a Jhereg or a Dragon. To her, you were either living or dead, and she got along better with you if you were dead.

I asked her, "Did you know Baritt?"

She nodded absently.

"Do you know if he was working with anyone shortly before his death?"

She shook her head, just as absently.

"Well, uh, thanks," I said, and moved on.

"Vladimir," said Cawti, "what's this business with Baritt all about?"

"I think someone is backing up Laris—someone big, probably in the House of the Dragon. I think whoever it is was working with Baritt at some point. I'm trying to find out who."

I took her to a corner and pulled out the list Fentor had handed me. There were seven names on it. None of them meant anything to me.

"Recognize any of the names?"

"No. Should I?"

"Descendants of Baritt. I'm going to have to check them out, I think."

"Why?"

I gave her a rundown on the story of the riot. Her beautiful face drew up into an ugly sneer. She said, "If I'd known what he had in mind—"

"Laris?"

She didn't answer.

"Why take it so hard?" I asked her.

She stared at me. "Why take it so hard? He's using our people. That's us, Easterners, being set up to be beaten and killed just to manipulate a few guards. What do you mean, why take it so hard?"

"How long have you lived in the Empire, Cawti?"

"All my life."

I shrugged. "I don't know. I guess I'm used to it, that's all. I expect things like that."

She looked at me coldly. "It doesn't bother you anymore, eh?"

I opened and shut my mouth a couple of times. "It still bothers me, I guess, but . . . Deathsgate, Cawti. You know what kind of people live in those areas. I got out of it, and you got out of it. Any of them—"

"Crap. Don't start on that. You sound like a pimp. 'I don't use 'em any more than they want to be used. They can do something else if they want. They like working for me.' Crap. I suppose you feel the same way about slaves, right? They must like it or they'd run away."

To be honest, it had never occurred to me to think about it. But Cawti was looking at me with rage in her lovely brown eyes. I felt a sudden flash of anger and said, "Look, damn it, *I've* never 'worked' on an Easterner, remember, so don't give me any—"

"Don't throw that up at me," she snapped. "We've been over it once. I'm sorry. But it was a job, all right? That has nothing to do with your not caring about what happens to our own people." She kept glaring at me. I've been glared at by experts, but this was different. I opened my mouth to say something about what it had to do with, but I couldn't. It suddenly hit me that I could *lose* her, right now. It was like walking into a tavern where you're going to finalize someone, and realizing that the guy's bodyguards might be better than you. Except then, all you're liable to lose is your life. As I stood there, I realized what I was on the verge of losing.

"Cawti," I started to say, but my voice cracked. She turned away. We stood like that, in a corner of Morrolan's dining room, with multitudes of Dragaerans around us, but we might as well have been in our own universe.

How long we stood there I don't know. Finally, she turned back to me and said, "Forget it, Vlad. Let's just enjoy the party."

I shook my head. "Wait."

"Yes?"

I took both of her hands, turned her around, and led her

into a small alcove off to the side of the main room. Then I took both of her hands again and said, "Cawti, my father ran a restaurant. The only people who came in were Teckla and Jhereg, because no one else would associate with us. My father, may the Lords of Judgment damn his soul for a thousand years, wouldn't let me associate with Easterners because he wanted to be accepted as Dragaeran. You, maybe, got a title after you'd made some money, so you could get a link to the Orb. I was given a title through my father, who spent our life savings on it, because he wanted to be accepted as Dragaeran.

"My father tried to make me learn Dragaeran swordsmanship, because he wanted to be accepted as Dragaeran. He tried to prevent me from studying witchcraft, because he wanted to be accepted as Dragaeran. I could go on for an hour. Do you think we were ever accepted as Dragaeran? Crap. They treated us like teckla droppings. The ones that didn't despise us because we were Easterners hated us because we were Jhereg. They used to catch me, when I went on errands, and bash me around until—never mind."

She started to say something, but I cut her off. "I don't doubt that you could tell me stories just as bad; that isn't the point." My voice dropped to a whisper. "I hate them," I said, squeezing her hands until she winced. "I joined the organization as muscle so I could get paid for beating them up, and I started 'working' so I could get paid for killing them. Now I'm working my way up the organization so I can have the power to do what I want, by my own rules, and maybe show a few of them what happens when they underrate Easterners.

"There are exceptions—Morrolan, Aliera, Sethra, a few others. For you, maybe Norathar. But they don't matter. Even when I work with my own employees, I have to ignore how much I despise them. I have to make myself pretend I don't want to see every one of them torn apart. Those friends I mentioned—the other day, they were discussing conquering the East, right in front of me, as if I wouldn't care."

I paused and took a deep breath.

"So I have to not care. I have to *convince* myself that I don't care. That's the only way I can stay sane; I do what I have to do. And there's precious little pleasure in this life, except the satisfaction of setting a goal, worthwhile or not, and meeting it.

"How many people can you trust, Cawti? I don't mean trust not to stab you in the back, I mean *trust*—trust with your soul? How many? Up until now, Loiosh has been the only one I could share things with. Without him, I'd have gone out of my head, but we can't really talk as equals. Finding you has . . . I don't know, Cawti. I don't want to lose you, that's all. And not for something as stupid as this."

I took another deep breath.

"I talk too much," I said. "That's all I wanted to say."

While I'd been speaking, her face had relaxed, the rage draining out of it. When I finished, she came into my arms and held me, rocking me gently.

"I love you, Vladimir," she said softly.

I buried my face in her neck and let the tears come.

Loiosh nuzzled my neck. I felt Cawti scratching his head.

A bit later, after I'd recovered, Cawti brushed my face with her hands and Loiosh licked my ear. We walked back to face the multitude. Cawti placed her hand on my left arm as we walked; I covered it with my right hand and squeezed.

I noticed the Sorceress in Green, but avoided her, not feeling like a confrontation just then. I looked for Morrolan, but didn't see him. I noticed the Necromancer talking to a tall, dark-haired Dragaeran woman. The latter turned for a moment, and I was suddenly struck by her resemblance to Sethra Lavode. I wondered. . . .

"Excuse me," I said, approaching them. They broke off and looked at me. I bowed to the stranger. "I am Vladimir Taltos, House Jhereg. This is the Dagger of the Jhereg. May I ask whom I have the honor of addressing?"

"You may," she said.

I waited. Then I smiled and said, "Whom do I have the honor of addressing?"

"I am Sethra," she said. Bingo!

"I have heard much of you from your namesake," I told her.

"No doubt. If that is all you wish to say, I am engaged just at the moment."

"I see," I said politely. "As a matter of fact, if you can spare a few moments—"

"My dear Easterner," she said, "I am aware that Sethra Lavode, for reasons best known to herself, chooses to tolerate your presence, but I am no longer apprenticed to her, so I see no reason why I should. I have no time for Easterners, and no time for Jhereg. Is all of this clear to you?"

"Quite." I bowed once more; Cawti did the same. Loiosh hissed at her as we turned away.

"Friendly, isn't she?"

"Quite," said Cawti.

At that moment Morrolan came in, escorting Norathar. She was dressed in black and silver, the colors of the House of the Dragon. I looked at Cawti; her face was expressionless. We approached them, fighting our way through the crowd.

Norathar and Cawti locked eyes, and I couldn't see what was passing between them. But then they smiled, and Cawti said, aloud, "The colors are most fetching. You wear them well."

"Thank you," said Norathar softly. I noticed that there was a ring on the little finger of her right hand. On its face was a dragon, with two red eyes.

I turned to Morrolan. "Is it official?"

"Not yet," he said. "Aliera is speaking to the Dragon Council about setting up an inquiry. It may take a few more days."

I looked back at Norathar and Cawti, who were talking a few paces away from us. Morrolan was silent. It is a very rare skill in a man, and far more rare in an aristocrat, to know when to be still, but Morrolan had it. I shook my head as I watched Cawti. First, I'd become angry with her, then I had poured out my problems at her feet; when all the time her partner of—how long?—at least five years, was on the verge of becoming a Dragonlord.

By the Demon Goddess! What Cawti must have gone through as a child would have been very much like what I went through, or worse. Her friendship with Norathar must have been like my relationship with Loiosh, and she was watching it end. Gods, but I can be an insensitive ass when I try!

I looked at Cawti then, from behind and to the side. I'd never really *looked* at her before. As any man with the least amount of experience can tell you, looks mean absolutely nothing as far as bedding is concerned. But Cawti would have been attractive by the standards of any human. Her ears were round, not the least bit pointed, and she had no trace of facial hair. (Contrary to some Dragaerans' belief, only male Easterners have whiskers—I don't know why.) She was smaller than I, but she had long legs that made her seem taller than she was. A thin face, almost hawklike, and piercing brown eyes. Hair was black, perfectly straight, falling below her shoulders. She obviously paid a fair amount of attention to it, because it glistened in the light and was cut off exactly even.

Her breasts were small, but firm. Her waist, slender. Her buttocks were also small, and her legs slim but well muscled. Most of this, you understand, I was remembering rather than seeing, but as I looked, I decided that, even on this level, I'd done rather well for myself. A crude way of putting it, I suppose, but—

She turned away from Norathar and caught me looking at her. For some reason, this pleased me. I held out my left arm as she came up; she pressed it. I reached for contact with her and it came more easily than last time.

"Cawti . . ."

"It's all right, Vladimir."

Norathar came up to us then, and said, "I'd like a word with you, Lord Taltos."

"Call me 'Vlad.'"

"As you wish. Excuse us," she said to the others, and we walked a bit away.

Before she could say anything I started in. "If you're

going to give me any of the don't-you-dare-hurt-her dung, you can forget it."

She gave me a thin smile. "You seem to know me," she said. "But why should I forget it? I mean it, you know. If you hurt her needlessly, I'll kill you. I just feel I should tell you that."

"The wise falcon hides his claws," I said, "and it's the poor assassin who warns his target."

"Are you trying to make me angry with you, Vlad? I care about Cawti. I care enough to destroy anyone who causes her pain. I feel I should let you know, so you can avoid doing it."

"How kind of you. What about you? Haven't you hurt her more than I ever could?"

To my surprise, she didn't even start to get angry. She said, "It may look that way, and I know I've hurt her, but not as badly as you could. I've seen the way she looks at you."

I shrugged. "I don't see that it matters," I said. "The way things are looking, I'm liable to be dead in a week or two anyway."

She nodded, but didn't say anything. She was, let us say, not overwhelmed with sympathy.

"If you really don't want her hurt, you might try helping me to stay alive."

She chuckled a bit. "Nice try, Vlad. But you know I have standards."

I shrugged, and mentioned something that had been bothering me for a while. "If I'd heard he was looking for you, I would have put everything on the line and hired you myself, and then I wouldn't be in this mess."

"The one who employed us didn't need to look for us; he knew where to find us, so there was no chance of your hearing."

"Oh. I wish I'd been so privileged."

"I have no idea how he found out—it isn't common knowledge. But it doesn't matter. I've said what I wanted to, and I think you under—"

She broke off, looking over my shoulder. I didn't turn around, just from habit.

"What is it, Loiosh?"

"The bitch you met last time. The Sorceress in Chartreuse, or whatever."

"Great."

"May I interrupt?" came the voice from behind me.

I looked at Norathar and raised my eyebrows. She nodded. I turned then, and said, "Lady Norathar e'Lanya, of the House of the Dragon, this is—"

"I am the Sorceress in Green," said the Sorceress in Green. "And I am quite capable of introducing myself, Easterner."

I sighed. "Why do I get the feeling that I'm not wanted here? Never mind." I bowed to Norathar and Loiosh hissed at the Sorceress.

As I walked away, the Sorceress was saying, "Easterners! I'll be just as pleased when Sethra the Younger goes after them. Won't you?"

I heard Norathar say, "Hardly," in a cold tone of voice, and then I was thankfully out of earshot. Then it hit me: I was looking for an Athyra who had been involved in the plot against Norathar. The Sorceress in Green was an Athyra. Just maybe, I decided. I'd have to think about how to verify or disprove this.

I returned to Cawti and said, "Is there anything keeping you here?"

She looked startled, but shook her head.

"Should we leave?" I asked.

"Weren't you going to be checking on that list?"

"This party runs twenty-four hours a day, five days a week. It'll wait."

She nodded. I gave Morrolan a bow, then we went out the door and down to the entryway without taking our leaves of anyone else. One of Morrolan's sorcerers was standing near the door. I had him teleport us back to my apartment. The sick feeling in my stomach when we arrived was not, I think, due only to the teleport.

• • •

My flat, at that time, was above a wheelwright's shop on Garshos Street near the corner of Copper Lane. It was roomy for the money because it was an attic, and the sloping ceiling would have annoyed a Dragaeran. My income, just before the business with Laris had started, had me thinking about getting a larger place, but it was just as well I hadn't.

We sat down on the couch. I put my arm around her shoulder, and said, "Tell me about yourself." She did, but it isn't any of your business. I'll just say that I was right in my earlier guesses about her experiences.

We got to talking about other things, and at one point I showed her my target in the back room, set so I could throw through the hall and give myself a thirty-foot range. The target, by the way, was in the shape of a Dragon's head. She thought that was a nice touch.

I took out a brace of six knives and put four of them into the left eye of the target.

She said, "Good throwing, Vladimir. May I try?"

"Sure."

She put five into the right eye, and the sixth less than half an inch off.

"I see," I said, "that I'm going to have to practice."

She grinned. I hugged her.

"Vlad," said someone.

"What the bleeding deviltries of Deathsgate Falls do you—Oh, Morrolan."

"Bad time, Vlad?"

"Could be worse. What is it?"

"I've just spoken to Aliera. She has found the names of the Lyorn and the Athyra who were involved in the test on the Lady Norathar. Also, you may wish to inform your friend Cawti that the Dragon Council has authorized an official scan for tomorrow, at the sixth hour past noon."

"All right. I'll tell her. What are the names?"

"The Lyorn was Countess Neorenti, the Athyra was Baroness Tierella."

"Baroness Tierella, eh? Morrolan, could Baroness Tierella be the real name of the Sorceress in Green?"

"What? Don't be absurd, Vlad. She—"

"Are you sure?"

"Quite sure. Why?"

"Never mind; I just lost a theory I liked. Okay, thank you."

"You are most welcome. A good evening to you, and I'm sorry you couldn't stay at my party longer."

"Another time, Morrolan."

I gave Cawti the news about Norathar, which broke the mood, but what was I supposed to do? I went into the kitchen and got us some wine, then got in touch with Fentor.

"Yes, milord?"

"House of the Lyorn, Countess Neorenti. House of the Athyra, Baroness Tierella. Are they alive? If so, find out where they live. If not, find out how they died. Get right on it."

"Yes, milord."

Cawti sighed.

"I'm done," I said quickly. "It was just—"

"No, it isn't that," she said. "I only wish there were some way I could help you with Laris. But all the information I have came from him, and I couldn't tell you that, even if it was useful."

"I understand," I said. "You have to live with yourself."

She nodded. "Things were so easy, just a week ago. I mean, I was happy . . . I guess. We were secure. My reasons for wanting to kill Dragaerans are the same as yours, and Norathar, well, she just hated everything. Except me, I suppose." I put my arm back around her shoulder. "Now, well, I'm happy that she has what she wants, even if she'd managed to convince herself she didn't want it anymore, but me—" She shrugged.

"I know," I said. Now, would you like to hear something crazy? I wanted, badly, to say something like, "I hope I can take her place for you," or maybe, "I'll be here," or even, "I love you, Cawti." But I couldn't. Why? Because, as far as I could tell, I was going to be dead in a little while. Laris was still after me, still had more resources than I did, and, most important, he knew where to find me, and I didn't know where to find him. So, under the circumstances, how could I do anything that would tie her to me? It was crazy. I shook my head and kept my mouth shut.

I looked up at her and noticed that she was staring over my shoulder and nodding slightly.

"Loiosh!"

"Yeah, boss?"

"What are you telling her, damn you?"

"What you'd tell her yourself, boss, if you weren't a dzur-brained fool."

I made a grab for him, but he fluttered over to the windowsill. I stood up, growling, and felt a touch on my arm.

"Vladimir," she said calmly, "let's go to bed."

Well, between wringing the neck of a wiseass, know-it-all jhereg, and making love to the most wonderful woman in the world—I mean, the choice wasn't hard to make.

13

"Well, what did you think I'd do?
Kiss him?"

"Milord?"

"Yes, Fentor?" I came more fully awake and pulled Cawti closer to me.

"I've located Countess Neorenti."

"Good work, Fentor. I'm pleased. What about the Athyra?"

"Milord, are you certain about her name? Baroness Tierella?"

"I think so. I could check on it a little more, I suppose. Why? Can't find her?"

"I've checked the records as thoroughly as I can, Milord. There has never been anyone named 'Tierella' in the House of the Athyra, 'Baroness' or anything else."

I sighed. Why does life have to be so Verra-be-damned complicated?

"Okay, Fentor. I'll worry about it tomorrow. Get some sleep."

"Thank you, milord."

The contact was broken. Cawti was awake, and snuggled closer to me.

"What is it, Vladimir?"

"More trouble," I said. "Let's forget it for now."

"Mmmmmmm," she said.

"Loiosh."

"Yeah, boss?"

"You are provisionally forgiven."

"Yeah, I know."

A few brief, happy hours later we were up and functional. Cawti offered to buy me breakfast and I accepted. Before we left, she wandered around the rooms, looking into nooks and crannies. She commented on a cheap print of an expensive Katana sketch of Dzur Mountain, sneered good-naturedly at some imitation Eastern cut glass, and would have continued all day if I hadn't finally said, "Let me know when you're through with the inspection. I'm getting hungry."

"Hm? Oh. Sorry." She gave the flat another look. "It's just that I suddenly feel as if this were home."

I felt a lump in my throat as she took my arm and guided me to the door.

"Where shall we eat? Vladimir?"

"What? Oh. Uh, anywhere's fine. There's a place just a couple of doors up that has clean silver and klava that you don't need a spoon for."

"Sounds good."

Loiosh settled on my shoulder and we went down to the street. It was about four hours after dawn, and a few things were just beginning to get going, but there was little street traffic. We went into Tsedik's and Cawti bought me two greasy sausages, a pair of burned chicken eggs, warmed bread, and adequate klava to wash it down with. She had the same.

I said, "I just realized that I haven't cooked a meal for you yet."

"I was wondering when you'd get around to it." She smiled.

"You know I cook? Oh. Yeah." She continued eating. I said, "I really ought to do a job on your background, just to make us even, you know."

"I told you most of it last night, Vladimir."

"Doesn't count," I sniffed. "Not the same thing."

Midway through the meal, I noted the time and decided to do some business. "Excuse me," I said to Cawti.

"Morrolan . . ."

"Yes, Vlad?"

"The Athyra you gave me isn't."

"I beg your pardon?"

"She isn't an Athyra."

"What is she, pray?"

"As far as I know, she doesn't exist."

There was a pause. *"I shall look into this and inform you of the results."*

"Okay."

I sighed, and the rest of the meal passed in silence. We kept it short, because being in a public restaurant without bodyguards can be dangerous. All it would take would be a waiter who knew what was going on to get a message to Laris's people, and they could send someone in to nail me. Cawti understood this, so she didn't make any comment when I rushed a bit.

She understood it so well, in fact, that she stepped out of the place ahead of me, just to make sure there was no one around. Loiosh did the same thing.

"Boss, stay back!" And, "Vladimir!"

And, for the first time in my life, I froze in a crisis. Why? Because all of my instincts and training told me to dive and get away from the door, but my reason told me that Cawti was facing an assassin.

I stood there like an idiot while Cawti rushed out, and then there was someone in front of me, holding a wizard's staff. He gestured, and then Spellbreaker was in my hand and swinging toward him before I knew what I was doing. I felt a tingling in my arm and knew that I'd intercepted something. I saw the guy in front of me curse, but before he could do anything else there was a dagger sticking out of the side of his neck. Whatever Cawti was doing, she apparently had time to keep an eye on the door. As I scrambled through, drawing a stiletto, I managed a psionic *"Help!"* to Kragar. Then I saw three more of them. Sheesh!

One was yelling and trying to fight off Loiosh. Another was dueling, sword to sword, with Cawti. The third spotted me as I emerged and his hand flicked out. I dived toward him, rolling (this is not easy with a sword at your hip), and whatever he threw missed. I lashed out with both feet, but he danced back out of the way. There was a knife in his left hand, set for throwing. I hoped he'd miss any vital spots.

Then the knife fell from his hand as a dagger blossomed from his wrist. I took the opportunity to roll up and do unto him what he'd been about to do unto me. I considered his heart an adequate vital spot; I didn't miss it.

A quick glance at Cawti showed me that she was doing all right against her man, who apparently wasn't used to a swordsman who presented only the side. I drew my rapier and took two steps toward the one Loiosh was engaging. He gave Loiosh a last swipe, turned to face me, raised his blade, and took the point of my rapier in his left eye. I turned back to Cawti. She was cleaning her weapon.

"Let's move, troops," I said, as Loiosh returned to my shoulder.

"Good idea. Can you teleport?"

"Not when I'm this excited. You?"

"No."

"How about walking, then. Back to my office."

Cawti cleaned her blade, while I dropped mine where it was. Then I led us back into Tsedik's and out the back door, and we began a leisurely stroll back to the office. If we walked fast, we'd attract even more attention than we already had, but I don't know if there is anything in the world more difficult than trying to stroll while your heart is racing and the adrenaline is pumping through your system. I was trembling like a teckla, and the knowledge that this made me an even easier target didn't help.

We had gone less than a block toward the office when

four more Jhereg showed up: Glowbug, N'aal, Shoen, and Sticks.

"Good morning, gentlemen," I managed. They all greeted me. I refrained from telling N'aal that he looked well, because he might have thought I was mocking him. He didn't seem resentful, though.

We made it back to the office without incident. I contrived to be alone when I finally lost my breakfast. It hadn't been that good, anyway.

I've known Dragaerans, and I mean known, not just heard of, who can eat a meal, go out and have an incredibly close brush with death, then come home and eat another meal. You might run into one of these jokers an hour later and ask if anything interesting has been happening, and he'll shrug and say, "Not really."

I don't know if I admire these types or just feel sorry for them, but I'm sure not like that. I have a variety of reactions to almost dying and none of them involves being plussed. It's especially bad when it comes as the result of an assassination attempt, because such attempts are, by nature, unexpected.

But my reactions, as I said, vary. Sometimes I become paranoid for a few hours or days, sometimes I become aggressive and belligerent. This time, I sat very still at my desk for a long time. I was shaken and I was scared. The sight of those four—*four*—kept running through my mind.

I was definitely going to have to do something about this Laris fellow.

"Time to get moving, boss."

"Eh?"

"You've been sitting there for about two hours now. That's enough."

"It can't have been that long."

"Humph."

I noticed Cawti was in the room, waiting for me. "How long have you been there?"

"About two hours."

"It can't—have you been talking to Loiosh? Never mind." I took a couple of deep breaths. "Sorry," I said. "I'm not used to this."

"You should be by now," she remarked dryly.

"Yeah. I've got that to console me. How many people do you know who have survived. . . ."

"Yes, Vlad? What is it?"

I sat there thinking for a very long time indeed. Then I asked the question again, in a less rhetorical tone of voice. "How many people do you know who have survived even two assassination attempts, let alone three?"

She shook her head. "There are damn few who survive the first one. I don't think I've ever heard of anyone surviving two. As for three—it's quite an accomplishment, Vladimir."

"Is it?"

"What do you mean?"

"Look Cawti, I'm good, I know that. I'm also lucky. But I'm not *that* good, and I'm not *that* lucky. What does that leave?"

"That the assassins were incompetent?" she said, raising an eyebrow.

I saw it and raised one. "Are you?"

"No."

"So what else does it leave?"

"I give up. What?"

"That the attempts weren't real."

"What?"

"What if Laris hasn't been trying to kill me?"

"That's absurd."

"I agree. But so is surviving three assassination attempts."

"Well, yes, but—"

"Let's think about it, all right?"

"How can I think about it? Damn it, I did one of them myself."

"I know. All right, we'll start with you, then. Were you actually hired to assassinate me, or were you hired to make it look like you were trying to assassinate me?"

"Why on Dragaera—?"

"Don't evade the issue, please. Which was it?"

"We were hired to assassinate you, damn it!"

"That's admissible at Court, you know. Never mind," I said quickly as she started flushing. "Okay, you say you were hired to assassinate me. Suppose you were given the job of making it look good. How—"

"I wouldn't take it. And get myself killed?"

"Skip that for the moment. Just suppose. How would you deal with the questions I've been asking, if your job was to make me think Laris wanted to kill me?"

"I—" she stopped and looked puzzled.

"Right. You'd answer just as you've been answering."

"Vladimir," she said slowly, "do you actually think that's the case?"

"Uh . . . not really. But I have to allow for the possibility. Don't I?"

"I guess," she said. "But where does that leave you?"

"It means that, for the moment, we can forget about you and Norathar."

"You still haven't said *why* he'd want to do this."

"I know. Skip that, too. Let's take the attempt outside the office. I've told you about it, right?"

"Yes."

"Okay. I got out of that because I'm quick and accurate and, mostly, because Loiosh warned me in time, and took care of one of them so that I was free to deal with the other."

"I was wondering if you'd remember that, boss."

"Shut up, Loiosh."

"Now," I continued, "how could Laris, and therefore anyone he hired, *not* have known about Loiosh?"

"Well, of course he knew about him—that's why he sent two assassins."

"But they underestimated him?"

"Well—forgive me, Loiosh—but he didn't do all that well against Norathar and me. Also, you reacted better and more quickly than Laris could have expected. As I told you before, Vladimir, you have a talent for making people underestimate you."

"Maybe. Or maybe he gave the job to a pair of incompetents, hoping they'd bungle it."

"That's absurd. He couldn't *tell* them to bungle it, that would be suicide. And he couldn't *know* they'd fail. As I understand it, they almost got you."

"And, maybe, even if they had, they wouldn't have made it permanent. We can't question them. Which reminds me, you could also have been told not to make it permanent. Were you?"

"No."

"Okay, skip that. Maybe he figured I'd survive, and, if I didn't, that I'd be revivified."

"But you still haven't said why."

"Wait for it. Now, about today—"

"I was wondering when you were going to get to that. Did you see what the one threw at you?"

"The sorcerer?"

"No, the other one."

"No. What was it?"

"A pair of large throwing knives, with thin blades. And they were perfectly placed for your head."

"But I ducked."

"Oh, come on, Vlad. How could he know that you'd react that quickly?"

"Because he knows me—he's studied me. Deathsgate, Cawti. That's what I'd do—what I've been trying to do as best I can."

"I have trouble—"

"Okay, just a minute then." I yelled past her. "Melestav! Get Kragar in here."

"Okay, boss."

Cawti looked an inquiry at me, but I held up a finger as a signal to wait. Kragar came into the room. He stopped, glanced at Cawti, and looked at me.

"This lady," I informed him, "is the Dagger of the Jhereg." As I said it, I looked a question at her.

"Might as well," she said. "It doesn't much matter anymore.

"Okay," I said. "She is also known as Cawti. Cawti, this is Kragar, my lieutenant."

"Is that what I am?" he mused. "I've wondered."

"Sit down." He sat. "Okay, Kragar. You're Laris."

"I'm Laris. I'm Laris? You just said I was your lieutenant."

"Shut up. You're Laris. You get word that I'm sitting in a restaurant. What do you do?"

"Uh . . . I send an assassin over."

"'An' assassin? Not four?"

"Four? Why would I send four? Laris wants to kill you, not give you Imperial Honors. With four assassins, you have three eyewitnesses to the thing. He'd get one good guy. There are plenty of 'workers' who wouldn't have any trouble finalizing you if they knew you were sitting in a restaurant. If he couldn't find someone good, he might go with two. But not *four*."

I nodded and looked at Cawti. "The way you and Norathar work keeps you out of contact with a large part of the Jhereg. But Kragar's right."

"Is that what happened, boss?" Kragar asked, looking puzzled.

"Later," I told him. "Now, let's suppose that you didn't have anyone around who could do it, or any two. For some reason, anyway, you want to use four of them. What do you tell them to do?"

He thought for a moment.

"Do I know where you're sitting, and what the layout of the place is?"

"Whoever told you I was there told you that stuff, too, or else you get back in touch with him and ask."

"Okay. Then I tell them that stuff, and say, 'go in there and do him.' What more is there to say?"

"You wouldn't have them wait outside?"

He shook his head, looking more puzzled than ever. "Why give you a chance to be up and moving? If you're sitting down—"

"Yes," said Cawti suddenly. "When I stepped outside,

they were just standing there, waiting. That's been bothering me, but I didn't realize it until now. You're right."

I nodded. "Which means that either Laris, or his button-man, is a complete incompetent, or—that's all for now, Kragar."

"Uh . . . good. Well, I hope I helped." He shook his head and left.

"Or," I continued to Cawti, "he wasn't really trying to kill me after all."

"If he was trying to fool you," she said, "couldn't he have done a better job of it? After all, you figured it out. If you're going to use success or failure to prove intention—"

"If we follow that reasoning, then I'm *supposed* to figure out that he's only bluffing, right? Come on, lover. We aren't Yendi."

"Okay," she said. "But you still haven't said *why* he'd only want to bluff you."

"That," I admitted, "is a tricky one."

She snorted.

I held my hand up. "I only said it's tricky—not that I'm not trickier. The obvious reason for him not to kill me is that he wants me alive."

"Right," she said. "Brilliant."

"Now, what reason could he have for wanting me alive?"

"Well, I know of at least one good reason, but I don't think you're his type."

I blew her a kiss and hacked my way onward. "Now, there are several possible reasons why he might want me alive. If any—"

"Name one."

"I'll come back to that. If any of them is true, then he might be hoping to scare me into making a deal. We might be hearing from him any time, asking me if I'll accept terms. If I do hear from him, what I say will depend on if I can figure out what he's after, so I know how *badly* he wants to keep me alive. Got it?"

She shook her head. "Are you *sure* you aren't part Yendi? Never mind. Go on."

"Okay. Now, as for reasons why he might want me alive,

the first thing that comes to mind is: he might not like something that will happen when I die. Okay, now, what happens when I die?"

"I kill him," said Cawti.

"One possib— What did you say?"

"I kill him."

I swallowed.

"Well," she said angrily, her nostrils flaring, "what did you think I'd do? Kiss him?"

"I. . . . Thank you. I didn't realize. . . ."

"Go on."

"Could he know that?"

She looked puzzled. "I don't think so."

Which suddenly made me wonder about something. *"Loiosh, could someone have—?"*

"No, boss. Don't worry about it."

"Are you sure? Love spells—"

"I'm sure, boss."

"Okay. Thanks."

I shook my head. "Okay, what I was *going* to say is, some of my friends—that is, my other friends—might come down on him. Not Aliera—she's the Dragon Heir, and the Dragon Council would have a lyorn if she started battling Jhereg—but Morrolan might go after Laris, and maybe Sethra would. Laris might be worried about that. But if so, why did he start the war? Maybe he only found out about my friends after it was too late to back out."

"That's quite a chain of supposition, Vladimir."

"I know, but this whole thing is a big chain of supposition. Anyway, another possibility is that he started the war knowing all this, but had some other reason for starting the war anyway, and hopes to get something without having to kill me."

"What reason?"

"What's the war about?"

"Territory."

"Right. Suppose that there is some particular area he wants. Maybe there's something buried around here, something important." She didn't look convinced. I continued.

"You saw the front of this place? They staged a raid on it. I didn't think anything of it at the time, but maybe my office is sitting right on top of something they want."

"Oh, come on. This is so farfetched I can't believe it."

"All right," I said, backing up a bit. "I'm not saying that I've hit dead center, I'm just trying to show you that there are possibilities."

She grimaced. "You aren't going to convince me," she said. "This whole thing is based on assuming that Norathar and I are part of the hoax. Maybe I can't prove to you that we aren't, but *I* know we're not, so I'm not going to be convinced."

I sighed. "I don't really believe you are, either."

"Well, then, where does that leave your theory?"

I thought about it for a while. Then, *"Kragar."*

"Yeah, Vlad?"

"Remember that tavernkeeper who tipped us off?"

"Sure."

"You said that he heard it being arranged—do you know if he heard someone actually talking to the assassins?"

"Yes, he did. He said the button-man addressed them by name. That's how I knew who we were up against."

"I see. When you went to see him, you said he was, how did you put it? 'Surprised and caught off guard.' Now, can you take a guess about whether he was more afraid of you, or afraid of being seen with you?"

"That's pretty subtle, Vlad."

"So are you, Kragar. Try."

There was a pause. *"My first reaction was that he was afraid of me personally, but I don't see—"*

"Thanks."

I turned back to Cawti. "Would you mind telling me where this thing was set up?"

"Huh?"

"You've admitted that you were hired to assassinate me. All I want to know is where it was arranged."

She looked at me for a long moment. "Why? What does this have to do with—"

"If my suspicions are confirmed, I'll tell you. If not, I'll tell you anyway. Now, where was it arranged?"

"A restaurant in Laris's area. You know I can't be more specific—"

"Which floor?"

"Huh?"

"Which floor?"

This earned me a quizzical look. "The main floor."

"Right," I said. "And a restaurant, not a tavern. Okay. And you didn't discuss it with him personally, did you?"

"Certainly not."

"So you don't even know who the job came from?"

"Well . . . not technically, I suppose. But I assumed—" She stopped, and her eyes grew wide. "Then who—?"

"Later," I said. "We'll get to that. It isn't what you think—I think. Give me a moment."

She nodded.

"Kragar."

"Yes, Vlad?"

"Our friend the tavernkeeper—I would like him to become dead."

"But boss, he—"

"Shut up. Finalize him."

"Whatever you say, Vlad."

"That's right. Whatever I say." I thought for a moment. *"Have Shoen do it—he's reliable."*

"Okay."

That's the trouble with not having any button-men: you have to do all the dirty work yourself.

14

"Lord Morrolan, I must insist."

I leaned back in my chair. "The next question," I said, "is why they— Cawti? What is it?"

She was staring at me through slitted eyes.

"He set us up," she said. "Or someone did."

"Hmmm. You're right. I was so involved in my problem that I didn't see it from your end."

"You said I was wrong before, when it occurred to me that someone else had done it. Why?"

"We got the information from one of Laris's people. That means that he must have had a hand in it."

"You're right. So it was him."

"But *why,* Cawti? Why does he want me to think he's after me?"

"I'll ask you another one," she said. "Why use *us?*"

"Well," I said, "it was certainly convincing."

"I suppose. When I tell Norathar about this—" she stopped, and a strange look came over her face.

"What is it?"

"I can't tell Norathar about this, Vladimir. She's the

Drågon Heir now, or soon will be. If she gets involved in Jhereg activities at this point, she'll lose her position. I can't do that to her. I wish I hadn't told her about the earlier attempt on you."

"Mmmm," I said.

"So it's you and me. We'll find that bastard, and—"

"How? He's vanished. He's protected against sorcery traces and even blocked against witchcraft. I know; I've tested."

"We'll find a way, Vladimir. Somehow."

"But why? What is he after?"

She shrugged, took out a dagger, and started flipping it. My breath caught for a moment, watching her. It was as if she were a female version of me....

"Okay," I continued, "what are the anomalies? First, hiring a team of assassins with the kind of reputation you and Norathar have, just to pull off a bluff. Second, doing it in such a way that you two find out and are still alive. He must have known that you wouldn't be pleased about this, and—"

"No," said Cawti. "The only reason I'm alive is that Norathar refused to speak to Aliera unless she revivified me. And the only reason Norathar is alive is that Aliera was convinced she was a Dragonlord and wanted to hear her story." She chuckled. "Norathar wouldn't talk to her anyway."

"I see," I said softly. "I hadn't known that. Well then, if this *was* his plan, he could have pretty much counted on you two being.... That's it, then."

"What?"

"Just a minute. Is it? No, that doesn't make sense, either. Why...?"

"What is it, Vladimir?"

"Well, what if the *point* was to kill you and Norathar? But that doesn't make sense."

She thought about it for a minute. "I agree; it doesn't. There are other ways to have killed us. And why continue the bluff after it failed?"

"I agree, but . . . could Laris know about Norathar's background?"

"I don't see how. I suppose it's possible, but why would he care?"

"I don't know. But look: the part of this that could most reasonably be a slip is that you and Norathar are still alive. So the only thing that *should* have been accomplished, so far, is the deaths of you two. Now of the two of you, it makes the most sense that someone would want Norathar killed, and it probably has to do with her background. What if we assume that's the case and go from there. What does that get us?"

"It still doesn't explain the war on you. Why not just kill her? Or, if he wants to be devious, give us the job of killing you and hire someone else to finalize us there?"

I nodded. "There's more to this than I can see," I admitted. "I know just the person we're going to want to talk to about it."

"Who?"

"What Dragonlord do you know of with the most interest right now in who the heir is? Who could have set this whole thing up, just to have Norathar dead, then revivified, then made the Dragon Heir? And maybe make attempts on my life just to make things look good? Who is it who most wants to find a new heir to the throne?"

She nodded. "Aliera."

"I'm going to arrange a teleport," I said.

Cawti and I leaned on each other for support. We stood in the courtyard of Castle Black, which floated above a small village about 175 miles northeast of Adrilankha. The tip of Dzur Mountain could be seen to the east, which was a more pleasant view than looking down provided.

"I'm sick," I remarked conversationally.

Cawti nodded.

"The couple that heaves together, cleaves together."

"Shut up, Loiosh."

Cawti chuckled. I glanced at her sharply.

"Loiosh, did you say that to her, too?"

"Shouldn't I have?"

"You shouldn't have said it at all. But that isn't what I meant. It's just . . . interesting."

By then our stomachs had settled down a bit; we approached the doors. They opened, displaying a wide hallway and Lady Teldra. She bestowed compliments upon us, during which we learned that Aliera was with Morrolan in the library. I told her we could find our own way. We went up the stairs, not stopping, as I usually did, to look at the artwork, and clapped at the door to the library.

"Enter," said Morrolan.

We did, and I could tell by looking at their faces that a remarkable thing was occurring: they weren't arguing about anything.

"Is one of you sick?" I asked.

"No," said Morrolan. "What leads you to ask?"

"Never mind. I have to talk to you, Aliera. Morrolan, this probably concerns you, too, so you may as well hear it."

"Sit down, then," he said. "Wine?"

"Please." I looked over at Cawti. She nodded. "Two," I said. "Where is Norathar?"

"She is being examined," said Aliera.

"Oh. Probably just as well."

One of Aliera's fine eyebrows climbed. "She shouldn't hear this?"

"Not yet, anyway."

As we pulled up chairs, a servant appeared with wine. Morrolan favors sparkling wines, whereas I think such things are an abomination. But, since he knows that, he brought a dry white, nicely chilled. I raised my glass in salute, sipped, and let my tongue enjoy itself while I tried to figure out how to tell Aliera what I had to tell her, and how to find out from her what I wanted to know.

When she'd had enough of waiting, she said, "Yes, Vlad?"

I sighed and blurted out the story of the assassination attempts as best I could, not going into any more detail than necessary about my own affairs, and never actually *saying* that Cawti had admitted trying to kill me. I mean, Aliera knew it, but habits are hard to break.

As I spoke, she and Morrolan became more and more alert. They occasionally exchanged glances. I finished up by saying that I could see no reason why Laris would have wanted Norathar dead, but I couldn't explain things any other way. Did they have any ideas?

"No," said Aliera. "But it doesn't matter. And, as soon as I can track him down, it will matter even less."

Morrolan coughed gently. "I would suggest, my dear cousin, that you at least wait until the Lady Norathar's position is confirmed. You are currently the heir, and the council hardly approves of Dragons involving themselves with Jhereg."

"So what?" she snapped. "What will they do to me? Find me unfit to be Empress? Let them! Besides, Norathar is certain to be confirmed."

"Hardly," said Morrolan. "She has a long history of associating with the Jhereg."

"Completely justified, under the circumstances."

"Nevertheless—"

"Nevertheless, I don't care. I'm going to find this Jhereg, and I'm going to show him Kieron's Sword. You are welcome to assist me. Hindering me would be an error."

She stood up and glared at Morrolan. "Well?"

I turned to Cawti and said in a normal tone of voice, "Don't worry about it; they do this all the time." She giggled. Neither Aliera nor Morrolan appeared to hear me.

Morrolan sighed. "Sit down, Aliera. This is nonsense. All I am asking you to do is wait a day or two, until we know the results of the council's decision on Lady Norathar. If she fails to become the heir, we will discuss it then. There is nothing to be gained by rushing out there like this. You have no way of finding him."

She glared at him for a moment longer, then seated herself. "Two days, then," she said. "At the most. Then I kill him."

"I'll help," said Cawti.

Aliera started to object, but Cawti interrupted. "It's all

right," she said. "You forget: I've worked with Dragaerans before. I really don't mind at all."

Cawti and I happily accepted Morrolan's hospitality in the form of a good lunch. Then I excused myself and went back into the now deserted library to think.

All of this business with Norathar, I decided, was fine, but it wasn't helping me find Laris, or at least get him off my back. Cawti and Aliera could talk about killing him, but they couldn't find him any more than I could, even if Aliera was telling the truth. And I couldn't afford to wait. If this kept up, I'd be out of business in a matter of weeks, at best.

It occurred to me that I might be able to get a message to him, proposing a truce. But he wouldn't go for it. And when I remembered Nielar's body, lying in the rubble of his shop, and the years I'd worked with Temek, and with Varg, I knew that I wouldn't go for it either.

Which brought me back to finding Laris, which brought me back to the big questions: Who had been working with Baritt shortly before his death? Was this person Laris's patron? How did this fit in with the business with Norathar? Was it Aliera? If not, who? And how to find out for sure?

I had reached that point when Cawti, Morrolan, and Aliera walked in. Before they could even sit down, I said, "Morrolan, did you find out anything yet about that Athyra?" I tried to keep an eye on Aliera as I asked the question, but her face betrayed nothing.

"No. Sethra is looking into the matter. Is there something in particular you wish to know?"

"Yes. You said that an Athyra is likely to be recommended by someone: can you find out who recommended the one used in Norathar's earlier examination?"

He nodded. "I see why you are asking. We must assume that the Athyra was, as you would say, 'a ringer,' and whoever recommended her may have known this. Very well, I'll see if I can find out. But I doubt that it was recorded, and it is unlikely that anyone remembers."

"Except the one who did it, of course. Hmmm. Is there

any way of putting together a list of everyone who *could* have made the suggestion?"

Morrolan looked startled. "Why—yes, that should be possible. I shall look into it immediately."

"Thank you," I said.

"It is nothing."

"How much will that help, Vlad?" asked Aliera after Morrolan had left.

"I don't know," I said carefully. "It's impossible in something like this to tell who's a willing dupe, who's an unwilling dupe, and who might be behind it. But if we can find out who made the recommendation, it'll at least be a start."

She nodded. "What about the Lyorn?"

"I haven't spoken to her yet. But look: I was told that the Lyorn was only there to make sure all the forms were followed. Say they were. There isn't any reason why the Lyorn couldn't have been taken in by whoever fooled Sethra the Younger about the first examination."

"True."

"So, of the people involved, we have: Sethra the Younger, who was duped or involved; the Lyorn, who was duped or involved; Baritt, who was duped or involved and then assassinated; and someone posing as an Athyra, or an Athyra using a false name."

"In other words, we have nothing."

"Right. We have to find out who that 'Athyra' was; she's our only clue to whoever is behind it—if, in fact, she isn't behind it herself."

"Well, Vlad, don't you have the name of the Lyorn noble? Why don't you ask her? She's liable to remember, or at least have written it down—Lyorns write everything down."

"Now there," I said, "is an idea." I considered for a moment. What would Aliera do if. . . . "But Lyorns don't like to talk to Jhereg," I said suddenly. "Is there any chance that you can find out for me?"

"What is her name, and where does she live?"

I told her.

"I'll find out for you," she said.

"Thank you."

She bowed to Cawti and me, and left.

"Why did you do that, Vladimir?"

"To find out what Aliera will do about it. If the Lyorn shows up recently dead, we have our answer. If not, we'll see what Aliera says the Lyorn told her." I sighed, and settled back to think. Cawti came up behind me and began rubbing my shoulders. I reached up with both hands and touched hers. She leaned over my head and kissed me upside down, dislodging Loiosh.

"You two are disgusting."

"Quiet. I'm busy."

There was a clap at the door. We sighed and Cawti straightened up.

"Come in," I called.

Norathar came in, death written all over her face. I stood up and glanced at Cawti, whose eyes were locked with Norathar's.

"The examination showed you aren't a Dragon," I suggested.

"Wrong," she said.

"Then what happened?"

"I am now confirmed as a Dragonlord—but not as the heir."

"Oh," I said. "I'm sorry. If you two would rather—"

"It isn't that," she snapped. "They wish to 'observe' me for a while before making me the heir. I have to serve a stint in the Phoenix Guard, to 'prove' myself. As if I have any desire to be Emperor, anyway!"

I shook my head. "Doesn't *any* Dragonlord ever want to be Emperor?"

"No," said Norathar.

"Okay. You're upset that they don't trust you enough to make it immediate?"

"Some. But I found out something else. I'm afraid that it isn't something I can discuss with you, Lord Taltos. But my sister and I—" She stopped, and I guessed that she and

Cawti were conversing psionically. After a moment, Norathar turned to me and said, "So you know."

"About why your attack on me failed? And what it means?"

"Yes."

"Yes."

"Then you'll understand why my sister and I must leave for the moment. We have to attend—"

"How did you find out?"

"I was told."

"By whom?"

"I swore not to say."

"Oh."

"Farewell for the—"

"Wait a minute, please. I have to think. There's something, before you go. . . ."

"Make it quick."

I ignored the looks of inquiry Cawti was giving me, and reached out—*"Morrolan! Come back here, quick!"*

"Why?"

"No time. Hurry!"

And then, *"Aliera, there's trouble. Morrolan's on his way, you should be here, too."* Whether Aliera was innocent or not, she would want to stop Norathar—I hoped.

Morrolan came bursting into the room, Aliera following by a second or two. Morrolan's blade was at his side, but Aliera was holding eight feet of glistening black steel. They looked at me.

"What is it, Vlad?" asked Morrolan.

"The Lady Norathar wants to go out Jhereg-hunting."

"So?"

"So the Dragon Council has—"

"This isn't any of your business, Lord Taltos," said Norathar coldly, her hand on the hilt of her blade.

"—accepted her as a Dragon, but—"

Norathar drew her blade. Loiosh hissed and gathered himself on my shoulder. I had a brief glimpse of Cawti, a look of anguish on her face, but then Morrolan's longsword,

Blackwand, was in his hand. He gestured with it toward Norathar, and her blade swung and buried itself deeply into a wooden beam against the wall of the library. She looked at Morrolan, wonderment in her eyes.

"My lady," he said, "at Castle Black, I do not allow the killing of my guests except under conditions where they can be revivified. Further, you, as a Dragonlord, should not have to be reminded of treatment of guests."

After a moment, Norathar bowed. "Very well," she said. She wrenched her sword out of the beam and sheathed it with the plain efficiency of a Jhereg, instead of the flash of a Dragonlord. "I'll be leaving then. Let's go, sister."

"Aliera, stop them!"

As I finished "speaking," Morrolan turned to Aliera. "What did you just do?"

"I put a teleport block around Castle Black," she said. "I hope you don't mind."

Norathar's eyes widened, then narrowed to slits. "Lord Morrolan," she said slowly, "I must insist—"

"Oh, for the love of Verra," I said. "Can you at least give me thirty seconds to finish my sentence?"

"Why?"

"Why not?"

She stared at me, but Dragonlords have been trying to stare me down since I was nineteen.

I said, "The Dragon Council wants to observe her for a while, before officially making her the heir. If she goes running off after Jhereg, that'll do it. I felt you two should know, and at least have the chance to talk her out of it before she does something that commits her. That's all. Now, the rest of you argue about it. I'm leaving before someone takes my head off."

I didn't quite run out of the library. I went down to the entryway and found a small sitting room. I helped myself to a glass of cheap wine and quaffed it, thinking dark thoughts.

The bottle was half empty when someone clapped at the door. I ignored it. It was repeated, and I ignored it again.

Then the door opened. My scowl died when I saw that it was Cawti. She sat down.

"How did you find me?"

"Loiosh."

"Oh. What happened?"

"Norathar has agreed to wait two days before doing anything, same as Aliera."

"Great."

"Vladimir?"

"Yes?"

"Why did you do it?"

"Do what? Stop her?"

"Yes. Don't you want someone to take Laris out?"

"She isn't going to have any better luck finding him than I will. The same goes for you and for Aliera."

"But, still, with more of us looking. . . ." She let the sentence die, and I didn't pick it up again. After a minute or so, I remembered my manners and poured her some cheap wine, too. She sipped it, delicately, thumb and forefinger around the stem, little finger off in space somewhere, just like at Court. And she kept her eyes fixed on me the whole time.

"Why, Vladimir?" she repeated.

"I don't know. Why ruin her chances for nothing?"

"Who is she to you?"

"Your partner."

"Oh."

She set the glass down and stood up. She walked over to my chair and looked down at me for a moment. Then she dropped to one knee, took my right hand in hers, kissed it, and rubbed her cheek against it. I opened my mouth to make some smart remark about was I supposed to pat her head, or what, but Loiosh brought his head around and smacked me in the larynx so I couldn't speak.

Then, still holding my hand, Cawti looked up at me and said, "Vladimir, it would make me the happiest of women if you would consent to be my husband."

About three hundred years later I said, "What?"

"I want to marry you," she said.

I stared at her. Finally I burst out with "Why?"

She stared back at me. "Because I love you."

I shook my head. "I love you, too, Cawti. You know that. But you can't want to marry me."

"Why?"

"Because, damn it, I'm going to be dead in a few days!"

"You said Laris was bluffing."

"Maybe he is, but he won't be if I keep coming after him. And whatever game he's playing, he *has* to make it real sooner or later."

"He won't get you," she said calmly, and I almost believed her.

I kept staring at her. Finally I said, "All right, I'll tell you what. When this business with Laris is over, if I'm alive, and you still want to, I mean, well, um, of course I will. I, oh, Deathsgate, Cawti. I don't know what to say."

"Thank you, lord."

"By the Lords of Judgment, get off the floor! You're making me feel like—I don't know what."

She calmly got up off her knees and stood before me. Then she broke into a grin, jumped, and landed on my lap. The chair went over backwards and we ended up on the floor in a tangle of limbs and clothes. Loiosh barely escaped in time.

Two hours and three bottles of wine later, we staggered back up to the library. Morrolan was alone there. I was just sober enough not to want him to know how drunk we were, so, somewhat regretfully, I did a quick sobering spell.

He looked us over, raised an eyebrow, and said, "Come in."

"Thank you," I said. I turned to Cawti, and noticed that she'd given herself the same treatment. A shame.

"Will you two be staying this evening?"

Cawti looked at me. I nodded. "I still need to check over that list of Baritt's descendants. Which reminds me, did you find out who might have recommended the Athyra?"

"One of my people is compiling the list. It should be ready by this evening some time."

"Good. I asked Aliera to find out about the Lyorn. Do you know if she did?"

"She is speaking to Norathar at the moment; I think they're attempting to determine how to locate this Laris person."

"Oh. Well, tomorrow, maybe."

"Yes. I'm having my dinner brought to me in the small dining room. I believe Aliera, Sethra, and Lady Norathar will be joining me. Would the two of you care to also?"

I looked at Cawti. "We'd be delighted," she said.

"Excellent. And, afterwards, you can join the party in the main dining room and continue your investigation."

"Yes," I agreed. "Maybe I can even avoid having any words with your Athyra friend."

"Athyra friend? I don't believe there have been any Athyra nobles present for some time."

"You know who I mean: the Sorceress in Chartreuse, or whatever."

Morrolan smiled. "The Sorceress in Green. I'll admit she looks like one, though."

Something went off in the back of my head. "She isn't?" I asked. "What is she then?"

"House of the Yendi," said Morrolan.

15.

"I imagine he's being well paid."

"What is it, Vlad? Why are you staring at me?"

"I can't believe what I just heard. A Yendi? Are you sure?"

"Of course I'm sure. What is it?"

"Morrolan, how many Yendi does it take to sharpen a sword?"

He looked at me through slitted eyes. "Tell me," he said.

"Three. One to sharpen the sword, and one to confuse the issue."

"I see." He chuckled a bit. "Not bad. What has that to do with our situation?"

"I don't know exactly, but—wherever you find a Yendi, you find a plot. A devious plot. Twisted, confusing, just the kind of thing we're facing. I don't know what it's about, but she—the Sorceress in Green—has been hanging around all of us since things started. She's been near you, near me, near Aliera, and indirectly near Norathar and Cawti and Sethra. All of us. This can't be an accident.

"And if that weren't enough, she looks like an Athyra.

We're sitting here trying to find an Athyra who doesn't exist, and now we find a Yendi who resembles one and who's been around the whole time. And you don't think she has something to do with all this?"

"I see what you mean," he said. "I think I shall speak to her, and—"

"No!"

"I beg your pardon?"

"Don't speak to her. Don't let her know, yet. The only advantage we have is that she doesn't know we're suspicious. We don't dare lose that until we know what she's after."

"Hmmm. It is axiomatic that no one but a Yendi can unravel a Yendi's scheme."

"Maybe. But to paraphrase Lord Lairon e'N'vaar, maybe I use different axioms."

He thought about it for a while, then said, "All right, Vlad. What's your plan?"

"I don't have one yet. First, I want to think over what we know and see if I can make some sense of it."

"All right."

"Cawti, why don't you find Norathar and Aliera?"

She nodded. Morrolan said, "You might need help," and the two of them went off.

I sat pondering for about half an hour, until the four of them returned, along with Sethra.

"Well," said Aliera, "what have you figured out?"

"Nothing," I said. "On the other hand, I haven't given up, either."

"Great," said Norathar.

"Sit down," I suggested. They all pulled up chairs around me. I felt like I was back in the office, with my enforcers sitting around waiting for orders.

"Vladimir?"

"Yes, Cawti?"

"Morrolan told Aliera about the Sorceress in Green. I didn't think to warn him not to."

"Damn. All right. So either the Sorceress is warned, or

Aliera isn't involved. I'm beginning to doubt that Aliera is behind this in any case. We'll see."

I said, "First of all, Lady Norathar, can—"

"You can drop the 'Lady,' Vlad."

I was startled. "Thank you," I said. I saw Cawti flash her a smile, and I understood. "All right, Norathar, are you sure you can't tell us how you found out what Laris did?"

"Yes," she said.

"All right. But think about it. If it was the Sorceress in Green—"

"It wasn't."

"Whoever it is, that person might be working with the Sorceress in Green, or perhaps is being used by her. I wish you could tell us who it is."

"Sorry. But I don't think it would help."

Cawti said, "Do you really think the Sorceress in Green is behind it?"

"Let's just say it's a real good guess. We won't know for sure who's behind it until we know what they're after."

Cawti nodded.

I continued. "Let's try to put the events in order. First, just before the Interregnum, someone decides that he doesn't want Lord K'laiyer to take the Orb. Maybe this someone is the Sorceress in Green, or the Sorceress in Green is working for him, okay?"

There were nods from around the room.

"Okay, the first thing he—or she—does is make it look like Norathar is a bastard. Of course, when confronted with this, K'laiyer fights, and, naturally, when fighting Sethra, loses. During the battle, they make sure K'laiyer ends up dead. This makes Adron the heir. So far, so good. Either that is what they wanted, or they didn't have time to deal with him. Because then we have Adron's Disaster, and two-hundred-some years of Interregnum. Still, nothing happens. Afterwards, Morrolan is the heir. *Still* nothing happens."

I looked at them again. They were watching me closely. I continued. "For over two hundred and forty years after the Interregnum, nothing. So whoever is behind it, if he is still around, doesn't object to Morrolan. But then, three years or so ago, Aliera shows up. Within a year Baritt, who is probably one of the conspirators, is assassinated. Two years after that, Norathar is set up, killed, revivified, and is suddenly going to be the heir. That's where we are as I see it."

Either Aliera hadn't caught any implication against her, or she was a fine actress. She seemed deep in thought, but not otherwise affected by what I'd been saying. Norathar said, "Vlad, is there any chance that the Sorceress in Green could have known Aliera well enough to know that we'd be brought back?"

I said, "Uh . . . you mean, then, that even *that* was part of her plan? I don't know." I turned to Aliera.

She chewed her lip for a moment, then shrugged. "Anything is possible with a Yendi," she said.

"Not that," said Morrolan. We turned to him. "You are forgetting that I was there, too. If you are supposing that she set it up so that Aliera would kill, then revivify, Norathar, then she must have known that I would be with Aliera. I will not believe that she could predict exactly where we would have been standing when we teleported, and if I had happened to be closer to Norathar than Aliera was, I'd have attacked, and I'd have used Blackwand."

Norathar paled as he said this. I swallowed and felt a little queasy myself. If Norathar had been killed by Blackwand, nothing and no one could have revivified her, nor would she have been reborn, as Dragaerans believe happens to anyone who isn't brought to the Paths of the Dead, and some who are. I wondered if Aliera could have arranged that. Or was Morrolan in on it too?

"You're getting paranoid, boss."

"Occupational hazard, Loiosh."

I cleared my throat and said, "I think we can safely assume that Norathar was expected to die permanently."

The others agreed.

"Now," I said, "let us turn to Laris. He may be well hidden, and well protected, but he is certainly losing money and taking big chances by not killing me. Why?"

"I imagine," said Cawti, "that he's being well paid."

"He'd have to be paid a lot to take that big a risk."

Cawti shrugged. "Perhaps he owes her a favor, or something."

"A big favor. Besides, I'm guessing that he killed Baritt as repayment of . . . wait a minute."

They all looked at me. Finally, Morrolan said, "Yes, Vlad?"

I turned to Cawti. "What do you know of Laris's history?"

"A fair bit. When I was studying you, I came across references to him from time to time, back when you both worked for Welok the Blade. And of course, I hear things now and then."

"Did you hear that he ran the war for Welok against the Hook?"

She and Norathar nodded.

"I was involved," said Norathar.

"Why did Welok let him run the war? And how did he win? He didn't have any experience at the time."

Cawti and Norathar studied me. "The Sorceress in Green?" asked Norathar.

I said, "It sure looks like he had something on Welok, or else knew how to get around him. What if our friend the sorceress maneuvered for him, and helped him with the war?"

Cawti said, "You think she's running the war against you, too?"

"Maybe. I met Laris, and he impressed me. I don't think he's a dupe, but I could be wrong. On the other hand, it's possible that the sorceress has something on him and can make him do what she wants. Especially if she can arrange for him to win in the end anyway, or tells him she can."

"If she has something on him," said Norathar, "why doesn't he just kill her?"

As a Jhereg, she was still a Dragon.

"Any of a number of reasons," I replied. "He might not know who she is. The hold might not disappear with her death. Maybe he can't reach her. I don't know."

"Any idea what that hold might be?" asked Cawti.

I frowned. "Could be anything. My first guess is that he's the one who finalized Baritt, and the sorceress has proof—easy enough if she had him do it, say as a favor in exchange for her help against the Hook."

"I can see it," said Cawti. Norathar concurred.

"This speculation is quite entertaining," said Morrolan, "but I fail to see where it helps."

"We're trying to understand what they're doing," I said. "Every detail we get helps put it together."

"Maybe," he said. "But I should like to hear your opinion on why the Sorceress in Green would do all this."

"Do what?" I asked.

"I'm not certain precisely what she's doing—"

"Exactly."

He nodded, slowly. "All right. I see."

I turned to Sethra, who hadn't said a word the entire time. "Have you any ideas, or guesses?"

"Not exactly," she said slowly. "But I'm beginning to suspect that the answer lies mostly before the Interregnum, the first time this conspiracy acted. What were they after, exactly?"

"Yes," I said slowly. "We should at least look into it." I glanced at Norathar; she looked like her teeth hurt. Well, I could hardly blame her.

"The motive for that one," said Cawti, "seems clear at least: it was an attempt to gain the Orb."

I shook my head. "I've been told that no Dragon wants the Orb."

"What about Adron?" she asked, looking at Aliera.

Aliera smiled. "A point," she said. "But my father didn't really want the Orb, he was forced to make a try for it out of a sense of duty."

I stared at her. "Wait a minute. Did your father know the Sorceress in Green?"

Aliera looked startled. "I . . . believe they were acquainted, yes. But if you're thinking that my father was the one behind the whole thing—"

"I wouldn't say I *think* so; I'm just checking into it."

She glared at me, and her eyes turned to steely gray. "If you feel you must."

"I feel I must. How well acquainted were they?"

"They often saw each other, and Sethra, at Dzur Mountain. Ask Sethra. She knows better than I."

I turned to Sethra. "Well?"

"I doubt," she said, "that Adron was behind a conspiracy of this type. It isn't his style. Besides, he and Baritt got along quite well."

"That proves nothing," I said. "Or, if anything, it makes the case stronger against him. How well did he get along with the Sorceress in Green?"

Sethra closed her eyes, as if having trouble remembering. Then she said, "We all got along in those days. Adron was never especially close to the sorceress, though."

"So," I said, "if Adron felt it his duty to take the Orb, he might have felt it was his duty to make sure *he* was the next Dragon Emperor."

"I don't believe it," snapped Aliera, becoming more angry by the minute. I started laughing. She stood up, glaring. "Mind letting me in on the joke, Vlad?"

"I just can't help but see how funny it is. We're talking about a guy who, trying to take the Orb, blew up half the Dragaeran Empire, created a Sea of Chaos where the biggest city in the Empire used to be, killed I don't know how many millions of people, and you're upset because I'm wondering if he faked a bit of evidence to make his path a little easier."

Cawti started laughing, too. None of the others seemed to think it was funny. That made it even funnier, and, for a moment, I almost had hysterics. Aliera said, "That's different. This involved tricking Sethra, who was a friend. There is such a thing as honor in the House of the Dragon."

Strangely, that sobered me up. It wasn't any less funny, but, in a way, it was sad, too. Presently Cawti got the better of her mirth. I said, "All right, Aliera. Maybe he didn't do it himself, but the Sorceress in Green could have done it without his knowledge, couldn't she?"

Aliera sat down again and sniffed. "I doubt it."

"All right, then, how did Adron and Norathar's father, K'laiyer, get along?"

Aliera shrugged and looked away haughtily. I turned to Sethra. She looked uncomfortable, but said, "They had disagreements, I remember. They weren't bitter enemies, by any means, but they did disagree."

"Of course they disagreed!" said Aliera. "My father felt the Dragons had to take the throne, K'laiyer didn't."

Sethra nodded. "That was pretty much it," she said. "They didn't agree on how immediate the problem was."

"What problem?"

"The decadence of the Emperor. Phoenix Emperors always become decadent at the end of their reign, except every seventeenth Cycle, when we have a reborn Phoenix, such as Zerika. Since that was at the end of the Great Cycle—seventeen Cycles—it was especially bad. The Empire appeared to be falling apart, there were Easterners making encroachments on the eastern border, and Adron felt the Emperor should either step down or be removed."

"And K'laiyer didn't?"

"No. I remember him pointing out to me that the 'encroachments' were into territories where most of the population was made up of Easterners anyway. He said that it was basically their land, and he saw no reason why they shouldn't have it back."

"I think I would've liked the guy," I said.

"Maybe," said Sethra. "He was likeable enough. And he would have made a good Emperor, I think."

"It sounds to me," I said, looking at Aliera, "as if Adron was—"

"I believe it is time to dine," said Morrolan. "Perhaps we should continue this after the meal?"

I smiled a bit, nodded, stood, and offered Cawti my arm. She took it, and we headed toward the small dining room. I hoped this meal would be easier to digest than the last one with this crowd.

Which set me to remembering that meal. Which set me

to remembering the days I had spent in Dzur Mountain. Most of the memories were quite pleasant.

But I remembered one conversation. . . . *That* couldn't have anything to do with this. Could it? The whole thing, just to accomplish *that?* But then, Dragaerans are Dragaerans.

"Wait a minute."

Morrolan sighed and turned around. "Yes, Vlad?"

"I just—"

"Can it wait?"

"Uh . . . let's go in and sit down while I think about it." My mind was racing like a cat-centaur. I think I bumped into a few people and walls as I found my place.

I noticed that we were sitting in exactly the same positions that we'd been in before. A servant brought wine. I drank some without tasting it.

"All right, Vlad," said Morrolan, in a resigned tone of voice. "What is it?"

"I think I might have just figured out who's behind this, and why."

I suddenly had everyone's attention.

"Go on," said Morrolan.

"Verra, but this is convoluted. But, with the Sorceress in Green doing the planning, how could it not be?"

"Well, who is it?"

"Let me put it this way: I'm going to guess that, between two and three years ago, the Sorceress in Green had a falling out with a certain individual she'd been friendly with up until then."

I turned to Sethra. "Am I right?"

She looked puzzled. Then, suddenly, her nostrils flared and her eyes widened. After a moment, she nodded.

"That's it, then."

"What, Vlad?" said Morrolan, still calm.

"You're enjoying keeping everyone in suspense, aren't you, boss?"

"Shut up, Loiosh."

"Okay, I'll put it this way: Suppose Norathar has just

been killed. By Morrolan and Aliera. End of problem. So, the correct heir to the throne is out of the way, right? Who's next?"

"Aliera," said Morrolan.

"Right. But information comes out that she was involved in a Jhereg war. Then what?"

"Mmmmm," said Morrolan. "The council might—"

"Assume further that the council is being manipulated. Maybe just a bit, maybe a lot, but there are strings being pulled."

"All right, so Aliera is out as heir, if that's what you want."

"Right. And, by the same logic, Morrolan, so are you. Who's next?"

They looked at each other. "I don't know," said Aliera at last.

"Neither do I. But, in a sense, it doesn't matter. I'm sure the Sorceress in Green knows. Whoever it is probably isn't even involved—it's merely someone whose politics are known. No Dragon wants to be heir, you said. What does every Dragon want to be?"

"Warlord," said Aliera, with no hesitation.

"Right. Morrolan, why don't you send for that list, if it's ready now."

"But . . . all right." He concentrated for a moment. "It's on the way."

"What list?" asked Sethra.

"I asked Morrolan to collect the names of everyone who might have suggested the Athyra wizard who helped on Norathar's scan.

"Now," I continued, "if Morrolan or Aliera were Emperor, each would have appointed the other Warlord, so you both had to go. Norathar had been harmless before, but with things moving as they were, it was safest to eliminate her, too.

"Before the Interregnum, there was an obvious choice for Warlord if Adron were Emperor, so—"

"Who?" said Cawti.

"I'll get to it. Anyway, without his knowledge, it was

arranged for him to become the heir. When he failed, the Phoenix remained in power, so there was no immediate problem. Then Morrolan became the heir, which was fine—"

"It was?" said Morrolan.

"Yes—until Aliera suddenly arrived. Then, the person who *would* have been Warlord under you was out. And, worse than that, Aliera's politics were wrong. You both had to go. Baritt, who had been willing to help until then, drew the line at this. He had to go, too.

"So, the Warlord-to-be and the Sorceress in Green, who was a good friend as well as being a Yendi, laid new plans. The first thing they did was pretend to quarrel, so they wouldn't be linked in anyone's mind.

"The plan took two years to mature, which is quick work for a Yendi. The fact that you two became friendly with me, and that I moved up in the Jhereg so quickly, must have helped quite a bit.

"First, they were going to kill Norathar."

"Why?" said Morrolan.

"Because Aliera was looking everywhere for someone to be Dragon Heir instead of her. She wouldn't deliberately do something to get herself disqualified by the council; she wouldn't consider it honorable. But she was trying to find someone with 'purer genes,' or whatever it is the Dragons look for. That would have led her, eventually, to the e'Lanyas."

"It did," said Aliera. "I was trying to find out what had happened to Norathar already, just on the chance that she could lead me to another relative."

I nodded. "So they had to kill her, because, as soon as Aliera found her, she'd realize that she was, in fact, pure."

"All right," said Morrolan. "Go on."

"The idea," I said, "was to kill Norathar and discredit the two of you for helping me. I suspect that someone slipped somewhere, and you two were supposed to have been alerted sooner. I don't think they wanted to cut it as close as they did. But it worked anyway—until you, Aliera, spoiled everything by revivifying Norathar. Then they had to improvise. The first thing they did was to test Norathar, just to see if she could, in fact, be of use to them as Emperor."

"How?" asked Norathar.

"Don't you remember the Sorceress in Green asking you how you felt about invasion plans for the East? I didn't think anything of it at the time, but—"

"You're right!"

"Yes. And if you had said you were in favor, they would have stopped right there, finished me off, and found a way to convince you to make the right person Warlord. Since your politics were wrong, they tipped you off about Laris so you'd go rushing off to kill him—he's expendable—and disqualify yourself as heir."

Cawti shook her head. "But why continue the fake assassination attempts, Vladimir?"

In answer, I turned to Norathar. "If there hadn't been two failed attempts on my life, would you have believed that you'd been set up, even after you were told?"

Her eyes narrowed, then she shook her head. Cawti nodded.

At that point, right on cue, a servant arrived, holding a piece of paper. He gave it to Morrolan.

Morrolan glanced at it. "Find," I said, "the name of the person whom you would have named Warlord if Aliera had not shown up."

He did, and his mouth dropped open. Sethra leaned past Aliera and took the list from Morrolan's limp hand. She glanced at it, nodded, and threw it down onto the middle of the table, her eyes cold as the blade of Iceflame.

"I would rather," she said, "that she had tried to kill me."

There were nine names on the list. The third one down was Sethra the Younger.

16

"Vladimir and I will just watch."

We all sat there looking at each other; then Morrolan cleared his throat.

"Shall we eat?" he said.

"Why don't we?" said Sethra.

Morrolan gave the necessary orders. I have no idea what appeared, but I must have eaten it, because I have no memory of being hungry later.

"Will they be here tonight?" asked Norathar at one point.

Morrolan said, "I would expect them to be." There was no need to ask who "they" were.

"Then perhaps we should plan to meet with them. Do you agree, sister?" Norathar asked Cawti.

"Not here," I said. "Morrolan forbids the mistreatment of his guests."

"Thank you, Vlad," said Morrolan.

"You're welcome."

"But surely," said Aliera, "under the circumstances—"

"No," said Morrolan.

Before another storm could erupt, I said, "We should still verify all of our guesses before we do anything else."

Norathar looked at me. "You mean you aren't sure?"

"I'm sure. But it should still be verified."

"How?"

"I've a way. It may take a little time. But then, we're eating anyway."

"Fentor."

"Yes, milord?"

"Have you tracked down the ownership of those flats, yet?"

"No, milord."

"Maybe it'll help if I give you a couple of names that might tie into them. Sethra the Younger, and the Sorceress in Green."

"I'll check into it, milord."

"Very good. Get hold of me as soon as you have something."

"Yes, milord."

"With luck," I said aloud, "we'll know something soon."

"Vladimir," said Cawti, "how should we approach them?"

"Yes," said Morrolan dryly. "You wouldn't want her to turn you into a newt."

"I'll get better," I said. "In any case we can't attack them here if we want to do anything permanent to them. Does anyone know where the sorceress lives?"

"One never knows where a Yendi lives," said Sethra.

"Yeah. One possibility is Laris. If I can arrange to meet with him, I might be able to show him that his partners are stabbing him in the back. Maybe he'll help us set them up."

"But aren't you still going to try to kill him?" asked Aliera. "If you aren't, I am."

"And I," said Norathar.

"Sure I am, but *he* doesn't have to know that."

Aliera's eyes narrowed. "I will have nothing to do with such a plan."

"Nor will I," said Morrolan.

"Nor I," said Sethra.

"Nor I," said Norathar.

I sighed. "Yeah, I know. You insist that everything be honorable, upright, and in the open. It isn't fair to take advantage of someone, just because he's been trying to assassinate you and conspiring against your friends, right?"

"Right," said Aliera, with a perfectly straight face.

"You Dragons amaze me," I said. "You claim it's unfair to attack someone from behind, but somehow it's a fair fight even when it's against someone both of you know is weaker, less experienced, and less skilled than you. That's not taking advantage? What rubbish."

"Vlad," said Morrolan, "it's a matter of—"

"Never mind. I'll think of something—wait a minute, I think I'm getting that verification now."

I had a brief conversation with Fentor, then turned back to them. "It's confirmed," I said. "Sethra the Younger, through intermediaries, owns a row of flats that were used as part of the setup for the attempt on me by Cawti and her friend the Dragonlord."

"Very well," said Morrolan. "How do we proceed?"

"It is vain to use subtlety against a Yendi," said Sethra. "Make it something simple."

"Another axiom?"

She smiled coldly. "And I'll deal with Sethra the Younger myself."

"It's simple enough," I said a while later, "but Cawti and I aren't at our best right after a teleport."

"Cawti and you," said Aliera, "will have no need to do anything."

I looked at Cawti.

"I don't mind," she said. "Vladimir and I will just watch."

I nodded. I intended to do more than that, but there was no need to tell them about it. Except—

"Excuse me, Morrolan, but just to be safe, may I borrow a Morganti knife?"

His brows furrowed. "If you wish."

He concentrated for a moment. Soon a servant appeared with a wooden box. I opened it, and saw a small, silver-hilted dagger in a leather-covered sheath. I took it partway out and at once recognized the feel of a Morganti weapon. I replaced it in the sheath and slipped it into my cloak.

"Thank you," I said.

"It is nothing."

We stood up and looked at each other. No one seemed able to find anything suitable to say, so we just stepped out of the small dining room and walked over to the central part of the castle, where the main dining room was.

We walked in and spotted Sethra the Younger almost right away. Loiosh left my shoulder and began flying around the room, staying high enough to be unobtrusive. (Morrolan's banquet hall had ceilings that were forty feet high.) Morrolan approached Sethra the Younger and spoke quietly with her.

"Found her, boss. Northeast corner."

"Good work."

I gave this information to Morrolan, who began guiding Sethra the Younger that way. The rest of us converged on the Sorceress in Green; we reached her at about the same time Morrolan did. She looked at him, looked at Sethra, then looked at us. There was, perhaps, the smallest widening of her eyes.

Morrolan said, "Sethra the Younger, Sorceress, for the next seventeen hours you are not welcome in my home. After that time, you may return." He bowed.

They looked at each other, then at the rest of us. Others in the hall began to watch, sensing that something unusual was occurring.

Sethra the Younger started to say something, but stopped—the sorceress had probably told her psionically that it was pointless to argue. The two of them bowed.

Sethra Lavode stepped up behind her namesake and put a hand on her arm, above the elbow. They looked at each other, but their expressions were unreadable.

Then, abruptly, the Sorceress in Green was gone. Loiosh returned to my shoulder, and I looked at Aliera. Her eyes were closed in concentration. Then Sethra the Younger disappeared. Sethra Lavode left with her.

"What will she do to her?" I asked Morrolan.

He shrugged and didn't answer.

Presently Aliera spoke, her eyes still closed. "She knows

I'm tracing her. If she stops to break the trace, we'll have time to catch up with her."

"She'll find the most advantageous place she can," I said.

"Yes," said Aliera.

"Let her," said Norathar.

Cawti swept her hair back with both hands just as I was adjusting my cloak. We smiled at each other, as we realized what the gestures meant. Then—

"Now!" said Aliera.

There was a wrenching in my bowels, and Castle Black vanished.

The first thing that hit me was the heat—an agony of flames. I started to scream, but the pain went away before I had the chance. We seemed to be standing in the heart of a fire. From somewhere off to my left I heard a dry voice say, "Quick work, Aliera."

I recognized the voice as belonging to the Sorceress in Green. She continued: "You may as well dispense with your teleport block; I'm not going anywhere."

It occurred to me that she must have prepared herself while teleporting, then brought us into a furnace. Apparently, Aliera had figured it out and put a protection spell around us before we had time to be incinerated.

"You all right, Loiosh?"

"Fine, boss."

Then the flames surged around us and went out. We were in a room, about twenty feet on a side, with blackened walls. We were standing in ash that came above our ankles. The Sorceress in Green stood before us, her eyes as cold as the fires had been hot. In her hand was a plain wooden staff.

"You had best leave," she said coolly. "I am surrounded by my own people, and you can hardly do anything to me before they get here."

I glanced at Aliera.

The Sorceress in Green gestured with her staff, and the wall behind her collapsed upon itself. On the other side of it, I could see about thirty Dragaerans, all armed.

"Last chance," said the sorceress, smiling.

I coughed. "Are all Yendi so melodramatic?" I inquired.

The sorceress gave a signal, and they stepped onto the ash.

Aliera gestured, and we were surrounded by flames again for a moment; then they died.

"Nice try, my dear," said the sorceress. "But I'd thought of that already."

"So I see," said Aliera. She turned to Morrolan. "Do you want her, or the troops?"

"It is your choice."

"I'll take her, then."

"Very well," said Morrolan, and drew Blackflame. I saw the faces of the men and women facing us as they realized that he was holding a Morganti blade, and one of power that, beyond doubt, none of them had encountered before. Morrolan calmly walked up to them.

"Remember," I told Cawti, "we're just here to watch."

She flashed me a nervous smile.

Then there was a flicker of motion to my side, and I saw Norathar charge for the sorceress, blade swinging. Aliera hissed and leapt after her. A spell of some kind must have gone off behind me, because I heard a dull boom and smoke came billowing past.

The sorceress slipped past the front line of her troops and raised her staff. Fires leapt from it toward Norathar and Aliera, but Aliera held her hand up and they fizzled out.

Morrolan, Norathar, and Aliera hit the front line at the same instant. Blackwand cut a throat, swept across the chest of the next guard, and, with the same motion, buried itself high in the side of a third. Morrolan slipped to his right like a cat before anyone even struck at him, withdrawing Blackwand, then sliced open two bellies. He parried a cut and impaled the attacker's throat, then stepped back, facing full forward, slightly on his toes, blade held at head height and pointing toward his enemies. In his left hand was a long dagger. The room was filled with the sound of screams, and those who'd been watching Morrolan turned pale.

I saw three more guards at Norathar's feet. Aliera, meanwhile, was wielding her eight-foot greatsword like a toy, flipping it back and forth amid their ranks. She had accounted for five so far.

Then, incredibly, the dead guards began to stand up—even the ones slain by Blackwand. I looked at the sorceress, and saw a look of profound concentration on her face.

"Hold them!" cried Aliera. She stepped back a pace, held her blade with her right hand, and stabbed the air with her left. The corpses who'd been trying to rise stopped. The sorceress gestured with her staff. They continued. Aliera stabbed the air. They stopped. They started again.

Then Aliera did something else, and the sorceress cried out as a blue glow began in front of her. After a moment it went away, but I could see perspiration rolling down her face.

Morrolan and Norathar had ignored all of this, and by now more than half of the enemy had fallen.

I spoke to Cawti out of the corner of my mouth. "Should we do something?"

"Why? They're Dragonlords; they enjoy this kind of thing. Let them do it."

"There is one thing I'm going to have to do, though. And pretty soon, it looks like."

"What?"

About then Norathar broke through the line. The sorceress cried out and swung her staff, and Norathar fell over, clutching the air.

Cawti moved before I could do anything. She got through to her friend, somehow, and knelt by her side.

The ones who'd been fighting Norathar turned to Aliera, and she had to defend herself again. I took out a pair of throwing knives and, just to test, threw them at the sorceress. Naturally, they veered away from her when they got close.

I heard Morrolan curse and saw that his left arm hung uselessly at his side, and that there was red over the black of his cloak.

Aliera was still locked in some kind of struggle with the

sorceress while holding off three guards. There was a sudden flurry near her as two more of them came at her. There was an impossible tangle of metal, and three of the guards were down. Aliera was still up, but there was a knife sticking out of her low on her back, and a broadsword actually through her body, just to the right of the spine, front to back, above the waist. She seemed to be ignoring it; I guess sorcery is also good for overcoming shock. But no matter how skilled a sorceress she was, her gown was ruined.

Norathar seemed to be alive, but dazed. This, it appeared, would be the best chance I had. I drew two fighting knives, then ran forward as fast as I could through ash up to my calves. When I reached the fighters, I watched Aliera closely, then ducked under a swing. I left the knives in the stomachs of two fighters who had no ability to deal with an Easterner rolling past them; then I was beyond the line, about four feet from the sorceress. Spellbreaker was in my hand before I stood up, and I swung it in front of me.

She had seen me, of course, and greeted me with a gesture of her staff. I felt a tingling in my arm. I screamed, and fell over backward.

"Vladimir!"

"Stay there!"

I opened my eyes and saw that the sorceress had turned away. I smoothly got to my feet, drew the Morganti dagger Morrolan had lent me, came up behind her, and brought Spellbreaker crashing down on the back of her head.

The effect on her was minimal, since she'd had some sort of shield around her; she jerked a bit and turned around. But, while the shield had prevented the chain from hitting her, the chain had brought the shield down. Before she could do anything there was the point of a Morganti dagger against her throat.

Morrolan and Aliera were dealing with the last of her defenders, but Morrolan seemed unsteady on his feet and Aliera's lips were clamped tight with the concentration of holding herself together. Cawti was helping Norathar to her feet. I didn't have much time, so I spoke quickly.

"This fight isn't any of my business, and I'll get out of the way if you give me what I want. But if you don't tell me where Laris is, I'll cut your throat—with this. And if you warn him, I'll be after you as long as I live."

She didn't even hesitate.

"He's on the top floor of a warehouse on Pier Street. Two buildings east of the corner of Pier and One-Claw, on the south side of the street."

Shows you how much loyalty you can expect from the House of the Yendi. "Thank you," I said, and backed away, still holding the dagger and Spellbreaker.

She turned away from me, apparently taking me at my word. She did something that was probably putting her defenses back up. At that moment, however, Kieron's greatsword, in the hands of Aliera e'Kieron, swept the head from the last of the defenders.

Morrolan stepped forward, and a black streak came from the point of Blackwand and struck the sorceress. This, I was told later, took her defenses down again. And before she could do anything else, there was a sweep from Norathar's blade and the sorceress's staff went flying—and her right hand with it.

She cried out and dropped to her knees, and it was in that position that Norathar impaled her, directly through the chest.

There was dead silence in the room. The Sorceress in Green stared up at Norathar with a look of complete disbelief on her face. Then blood came from her mouth and she fell in a heap at the feet of the Sword of the Jhereg.

Cawti came up next to me. I nodded toward the three of them, standing around the body.

"Honor," I muttered, "in the House of the Dragon."

Aliera collapsed. Cawti squeezed my arm.

We returned to Castle Black, leaving the body of the Sorceress in Green where it was. I helped myself to a large glass of brandy, which I despise, but it's stronger than wine and I didn't want to suggest Piarran Mist; somehow this didn't feel like a time to celebrate.

"She was quite an accomplished sorceress," said Aliera weakly, from the couch where the Necromancer was working on her. There were nods from around the room.

"Vlad," said Morrolan, whose arm was in a sling, "what was it that you did to her, and why?"

"She had some information I wanted," I explained. "I got it."

"And then you let her go?"

I shrugged. "You said you didn't need my help."

"I see." I noticed Cawti holding a grin behind her hand. I slipped her a wink. Morrolan asked, "What was the information?"

"Do you remember that I'm in the middle of a war? Laris was backed by her, but he still has the resources to hurt me. He's going to find out that she's dead very soon. When he does, he'll start coming after me for real—I have to make sure the war is over before he does. I figured that she knew where Laris is hiding. I hope she wasn't lying."

"I see."

Cawti turned to me. "Shall we finish it up, then?"

I snorted. "Do you think it'll be that easy?"

"Yes."

I thought about it. "You're right. It will be." I closed my eyes for a moment, just to make sure there wasn't anything I'd forgotten.

"Kragar."

"Hello, Vlad."

"How's business?"

"A little better."

"Good. Get hold of the Bitch Patrol. In exactly two and a half hours, I want a teleport block to prevent anyone from leaving a certain warehouse." I told him where it was.

"Got it, boss."

"Good. In exactly one-half hour, I want the following people in the office: Shoen, Sticks, Glowbug, Narvane, N'aal, Smiley, and Chimov."

"Uh . . . that's all?"

"Don't be funny."

"Have we got something, Vlad?"

"Yeah. We've got something. And I don't want any mistakes. This ought to be quick, painless, and easy. So get everyone there, and make sure the sorceress you find is competent."

"Gotcha, boss."

The contact was broken.

Cawti and I stood up. "Well, thank you for the entertainment," I said, "but I'm afraid we have to be on our way."

Norathar bit her lip. "If there's anything I can do . . ."

I looked at her for a moment, then I bowed low. "Thank you, Norathar, and I mean that sincerely. But no. I think, for the first time in months, everything is under control."

We left them and went down to the entryway, where one of Morrolan's people teleported us back to my office. This time I made sure to warn them we were coming.

17

"You what?"

Now, I suppose, you expect me to tell you how I caught up with Laris after a long chase through the streets of Adrilankha, cornered him at last, how he fought like a dzur and I barely managed to kill him before he did me in. Right? Crap.

There were only two things that could have gone wrong. One, the Sorceress in Green might have lied about where Laris was, and two, she might have had time to warn him. But, in both cases, why? To the sorceress, he was merely a tool. And, since we'd discovered what they were up to, he was no longer a useful tool.

I didn't really think the Sorceress in Green had had time to warn Laris before Norathar finished her. And, if she had lied about where he was, there was no harm done. So I explained my plan to everyone in my office, which took about half an hour. I did make one point worth mentioning: "If anyone here has the idea that he can do well for himself by telling Laris about this, he can forget it. Laris had a backer; the backer is dead. Right now, we're holding nothing but flat stones, and he has nothing but round ones. So don't try to be clever."

I rummaged around my bottom-left drawer until I found a suitable weapon—a stiletto with a thin handle and a seven-inch blade. I put it into my belt on the right side. We sat around waiting for another half-hour, then Shoen and Chimov got up and slipped out the door. The rest of us waited ten minutes more, then stood.

"Luck, boss," said Kragar.

"Thanks."

Loiosh flew high above us as we set out toward Malak Circle. Cawti was leading. Sticks and Glowbug were to my right and left, and the others were walking in front and back.

We reached the circle and jogged over to Pier. We had almost reached Silversmith when I received a message from Shoen.

"He has four outside, boss. Two at the door, two making rounds."

"Okay. I'll send help."

"Thanks."

"Narvane and Smiley, run up ahead. Shoen is in charge of the operation. You have five minutes to get set up."

They ran off while the rest of us slowed to a casual stroll, hardly moving at all.

"Still clear, boss."

"Okay."

Cawti looked back at me and nodded. Six minutes later, Shoen reported in. *"All set, boss. It'll take between five and ninety seconds, depending on where the patrollers are."*

"Okay. Hold for now."

We reached the place on Pier where it curves, just before you get to One-Claw.

"How are they placed, Shoen?"

"If you give the word now, about thirty seconds."

"Do it."

"Check."

I held up my hand, and we stopped. I mentally counted off ten seconds, then we started walking again, quickly. We came around the curve and the building was in sight. The only people we could see were Shoen and Chimov. Presently, Narvane appeared next to them, then Smiley. We reached them a few seconds later.

I checked the Imperial Clock.

"The teleport block should be up now. Check it, Narvane."

He closed his eyes for a moment, then nodded.

I said, "The door."

N'aal said, "Maybe we should clap first."

Shoen and Glowbug stood by the door. They looked at each other, nodded, and Glowbug brought his mace down on the door mechanism just as Shoen set his shoulder into the middle. The door fell in.

N'aal said, "Won't you feel stupid if it was unlocked?"

I said, "Shut up."

Cawti slipped between them before we could move and stepped inside. There was a flurry of movement, and I heard the sound of falling bodies as Glowbug, N'aal, and Shoen went in. Loiosh landed on my shoulder as Chimov and Smiley stepped past the threshold. I followed, with Sticks and Narvane bringing up the rear.

It was a big, empty warehouse, with two bodies in it. Both had knives sticking out of them. We saw the stairs right away and took them. We didn't meet anyone on the way up. I left N'aal and Smiley to hold the bottom of the stairs to the third floor while the rest of us went up.

We emerged into a large, empty room. About five feet ahead of us were three smaller rooms; to the right, ahead, and to the left. Offices, I supposed.

Just as we got there, three Jhereg appeared from a room to the right. They stood there with their mouths hanging open. Sticks leapt at them, with Glowbug a little behind. Glowbug still had his mace, and he was grinning like an idiot. Sticks had his sticks. It took them about three seconds.

Then I sent Glowbug and Shoen to the right. I was about to send Chimov and Narvane to open the door ahead of us when I heard, "What's the ruckus about, gentlemen?" from the room to the left. I recognized Laris's voice.

I caught Narvane's eye. He stood in front of the door; the rest of us positioned ourselves behind it. Narvane raised his hand and the door flew in.

It was a small room, with about eight or nine padded chairs and two desks. One of the desks was empty; Laris was behind the other one. There were four other Jhereg in the room.

For an instant, no one moved. Then Laris turned to one and said, "Teleport."

We just waited.

The Jhereg he'd spoken to said, "There's a block up."

Cawti entered the office. Still none of them did anything. Sticks came in with his two clubs, then Glowbug with his mace. Then the rest of us.

Laris and I looked at each other, but neither of us spoke. What was there to say? I looked at his enforcers, most of them with half-drawn weapons. I told my people to stand aside. We cleared a path to the door. Sticks hefted his weapons, looked at Laris's enforcers, and cleared his throat.

He said, "No future in it, gentlemen."

They looked at the horde of us. Then, one by one, they stood up. They held their hands out, clear of their bodies. One by one, without a glance at Laris, they filed out.

I said, "All of you except Cawti, escort them out of the building." I drew the blade I'd selected.

When we were alone with Laris, I shut the door with my foot. Cawti said, "He's yours, Vladimir."

I made it quick. Laris never said a word.

An hour later I was staring at Aliera, my mouth hanging open. "You *what?*"

"I revivified her," she said, looking at me quizzically, as if to say, "Why should you find this unusual?" I was sitting in the library of Castle Black, with Morrolan, Cawti, Norathar, and Sethra. Aliera was on her back, looking pale but healthy.

I sputtered like a klava-boiler, then managed, "Why?"

"Why not?" she said. "We'd killed her, hadn't we? That

was enough humiliation. Besides, the Empress is a friend of hers."

"Oh, great," I said. "So now, she—"

"She won't do anything, Vlad. There isn't anything she *can* do. When we revivified her we did a mind-probe and wrote down the details of every plot of any kind she's ever been involved in, and we gave her a copy so that she knows we know." She smiled. "Some of them were rather interesting, too."

I sighed. "Well, have it your way, but if I wake up dead one morning, I'll come to you and complain about it."

"That's telling her, boss."

"Shut up, Loiosh."

Norathar, to my amazement, said, "I think you did the right thing, Aliera."

"So do I," said Sethra.

I turned to the latter. "Indeed? Tell us what you did to Sethra the Younger."

"The House of the Dragon," she said, "has decided that Sethra the Younger can never be Emperor or Warlord, nor can any of her heirs."

"Huh," I said. "But what did *you* do to her?"

She gave me a dreamy kind of half-smile. "I believe I found a suitable punishment for her. I made her explain the entire affair to me, then—"

"Oh? What did she say?"

"Nothing surprising. She wished to conquer the East, and complained to the Sorceress in Green, who was her friend, that when Lord K'laiyer became Emperor, he wouldn't authorize an invasion of the East. The sorceress came up with a scheme to make sure Adron became the Dragon Heir because they knew Adron would appoint Baritt to be Warlord, and Baritt was sympathetic to the invasion idea. Baritt agreed, mostly because he thought Adron would be a better Emperor than K'laiyer—sorry, Norathar."

Norathar shrugged. Sethra continued.

"After Adron's Disaster, they just let things lie. When Zerika took the throne and things got going again, Morrolan proved to be the heir. They arranged for Sethra the Younger to become friendly with Morrolan and found that he wouldn't object to an invasion, so they relaxed. When Aliera showed up out of nowhere and became the heir, they went back to work again. They came up with the idea of discrediting Aliera and Morrolan, using your friendship with Vlad. They already knew Laris, because he'd done some of the dirty work in arranging the fake genetic scan. When Baritt refused to cooperate, they had Laris kill him. Then they used that as a threat to make Laris attack you. Apparently he was perfectly willing to take over your territory, Vlad, but had to be convinced not to kill you right away. They told him he could have you after their plans were complete. You know the rest, I think."

I nodded. "Okay. Now, about Sethra the Younger . . ."

"Oh, yes. I had the Necromancer gate her to another Plane. Similar to Dragaera, but time runs at a different rate there."

"And she's stuck?" It seemed rather harsh to me—better to kill her. Besides, I wasn't nearly as upset with her as I was with the Sorceress in Green.

But, "No," said Sethra. "She can come back when her task is finished. It shouldn't take more than a week of our time."

"Task?"

"Yes." Once more, Sethra gave us her dreamy little smile. "I put her in the desert, with plenty of food, water, shelter, and a stick. And I set her to writing, 'I will not interfere with the Dragon Council,' in the sand, eighty-three thousand, five hundred and twenty-one times."

Picture an old man—an Easterner, almost seventy years old, which is a *very* impressive age for our race. But he's in good condition for his age. He is poor, but not destitute. He has raised a family in the midst of the Dragaeran Empire and done it well. He has buried (an Eastern term for "outlived"; I'm not sure why) a wife, a sister, a daughter, and two sons. The only surviving descendant is one grandson, who nearly gets himself killed every few weeks or so.

He is almost completely bald, with only a fringe of white hair. He is a large, portly man, yet his fingers are still nimble enough with the rapier to give a good battle to a younger man, and to shock the sorcery out of any Dragaeran who doesn't understand Eastern-style fencing.

He lives in the Eastern ghetto, on the south side of Adrilankha. He ekes out a living as a witch, because he refuses to let his grandson support him. He worries about his grandson, but doesn't let it show. He'll help, but he won't live through his children, and he won't live their lives for them. When one of his sons tried to make himself into an imitation Dragaeran, he was saddened and felt his son was doomed to disappointment, but he never offered a word of criticism.

I went to see this old gentleman the day after Laris's death. Walking through the filth in the streets made me want to retch, but I hid it. Anyway, we all know Easterners are filthy, right? Look at how they live. Never mind that they can't use sorcery to keep their neighborhoods clean the way Dragaerans do. If they want to use sorcery, they can become citizens of the Empire by moving into the country and becoming Teckla, or buying titles in the Jhereg. Don't want to be serfs? They're stubborn, too, aren't they? Don't have the money to buy titles? Of course not! Who'd give them a good job, seeing how filthy they are?

I tried not to let it bother me. Cawti tried too, but I could see the strain around the corners of her eyes and feel it in the purposeful way she walked. I should have felt good about coming back here—successful Easterner boy walks through the old neighborhood. I should have, but I didn't. I only felt sick.

There was no sign above my grandfather's shop, and nothing on display. Everyone in the neighborhood knew who he was and what he did, and he didn't care about anyone outside it. Dragaerans had stopped using witchcraft when the Interregnum ended and sorcery worked again.

As I walked under the doorway (no door), my head brushed a set of chimes and set them ringing. His back was to me, but I could see that he was making candles. He turned around and his face lit up in an almost toothless grin.

"Vladimir!" he said. He looked at me, smiled at Cawti, and stood looking at me again. He and I could communicate psionically (he had taught me how), but he refused to do so unless it was necessary. He considered psionic communication something too precious to use casually—though, as was his custom, he never criticized me for using psionics as I do. So we traveled when we wanted to speak with each other. And, since we had to pass through areas where Easterners walking alone are in danger, and since he refused to be teleported, he seldom left the area.

"Vladimir," he said again. "And who is this?"

Loiosh flew over, as if the question had been about him, and happily accepted some neck scratching.

"Noish-pa," I said, "I'd like you to meet Cawti."

She gave him a curtsy, and he positively beamed.

"Cawti," he repeated. "Do you have a patronymic?"

"Not anymore," she said. I bit my lip. Someday I'd ask her what that meant, but not now.

He gave her a kindly smile, then looked at me, his eyes twinkling and a thin, white eyebrow climbing a broad forehead.

"We'd like to get married," I said. "We want your blessing."

He came forward and hugged her, and kissed both cheeks. Then he hugged me. When he pulled back, I saw tears at the corners of his eyes.

"I'm happy for you," he said. Then his brows furrowed, for just a moment, but I knew what he was asking.

"She knows," I said. "She's in the same line of work herself."

He sighed. "Oh, Vladimir, Vladimir. Be careful."

"I will, Noish-pa. Things are looking better for me. I almost lost everything a while ago, but I'm all right now."

"Good," he said. "But how did you come to almost lose everything? That isn't good."

"I know, Noish-pa. For a while, the shadows were distracting me so I couldn't see the target."

He nodded. "But come in, have something to eat."

"Thank you, Noish-pa."

Cawti said, timidly (I think it was the only time in her life she's been timid about anything), "Thank you . . . Noish-pa."

And his grin became even wider as he led us inside.

The next day I moved into Laris's old office and set up business. I met with Toronnan, and set about trying to take control of the area Laris had been running—but that really belongs to a different tale. Besides, as I speak these words, I don't know how it's going to turn out, so I may not be telling you about it after all. I've still got word out for Wyrn and Miraf'n, and money to pay for their heads, so I expect that very soon I'll be seeing them—after a fashion.

The same day I moved into Laris's old office I finally got a chance to cook Cawti a meal. I have to say I outdid myself, too—goose with Eastern red pepper, Valabar-style kethna dumplings, anise-jelled . . . but you don't want to hear about that.

I will say, though, that while I was cooking, I came across an onion that had a small bad spot on the side. I cut the spot out, and the rest of the onion was perfectly fine.

Life is like that, sometimes.